Beauty in the Beast
A Shattered Fairytale

Tea Spangsberg

leaned her head against the cool wood, breathing deeply. She just needed a second before she had to face the world again.

"Belle?" an old voice asked behind her. She turned and smiled at old Mr. Tobias. He had been a traveling salesman but had settled in town when traveling became too hard on his body. He was the only place in the whole village you could buy a book. Or get help writing a letter. Mr. Tobias was Belle's saving grace. He had taught her to read and write and never cared about the scars marking her skin or the whispers following her around.

"Good morning Mr. Tobias." She gave him a smile.

He took her hand in his. "Happy birthday, my girl." He carefully padded her hand, the one with the scar. Belle couldn't help the tear breaking free, and she quickly wiped it away.

"So, are you here for your birthday book?"

"Yes, have you gotten anything new?"

"A few." He pulled out a few books from a shelf behind the desk and carefully placed them in front of her. She studied them each, but her eyes were drawn back to a smaller book with a blue cover. *La Belle et la Bête* was written in silver lettering on the front. It was the prettiest book she had ever seen. She carefully put it down. Such a lovely book was not something she could afford.

Mr. Tobias picked up the book and put it back in her hand. "From me to you, my dear. You know I would give it to you for free if you let me, but you will not, so I will take my usual price instead."

Belle wanted to refuse. The book was worth so

much more than the single silver coin she had in her pocket, but the draw of the book was too much. She handed him the coin and carefully tucked the book into the pocket of her dress.

With her prize safely stowed away, she made her way back to the house she shared with her father at the edge of the village.

It wasn't a big house, but it was warm and cozy. Being the blacksmith gave her father enough coin to feed them and care for them, and Belle was grateful that she had not been forced to marry. No man in the village would have her, and the outsiders who might show interest were always scared away by the rumors. Not that Belle wanted to marry anyone, but she longed to leave this place. This life. She touched the scars again. Unfortunately, there were just some things in life you could not escape.

She slipped into her bedroom and carefully pulled her new book out. She sat in the old rocking chair and opened the book to the first page. She didn't have much time; her list of chores was too long to spend much of her day idling around, but she could read that much.

"Belle?" Her father's deep voice ripped her out of the story, and she glanced around, worried. The shadows on the floor had moved, and she could hear her father move around the house.

"Coming, papa," she called and carefully placed the book on her little bookshelf beside her bed. It joined her most priced possessions, her twelve books. Her escapes.

Books by
Tea Spangsberg

Shattered Fairytales

Beauty in the Beast

The Tamora Andrews Duology

Dragonslayer

Dragonthrone

Stand Alones

Wicked Witch

The Reaper Comes Knocking

Chapter 1

The morning brought sunshine and the smell of freshly baked bread. Birds were singing in the trees, and bees buzzed around the flowers. Belle stood in the small garden behind her father's house, looking at the meadow that stretched all the way to the edge of the forest. The warm wind stirred the long grass, and gentle waves moved through it. It reminded her of going to the sea. Of a day spent with her feet in the cool sand, watching the water toss and turn. So beautiful and still so deadly. It had been her only wish on her birthday for as long as she could remember. Her little sister always wanted a new dress, but Belle wanted the sea.

But that was before. Before the monster took them. Before it killed her mother. Before. She touched her face, running her fingers over the uneven skin marking her features.

After, there had been no trips, no celebrations, and no happiness.

She turned away from the meadow and pulled up the hood of her cloak. It was too warm to wear, but she would rather be sweaty than have the people in the village stare at her like she was one of the monsters too. She should be used to it by now. After all, it had been almost fifteen years since they were taken. But it still hurt. It hurt when her little sister started pulling away from her. When people she had called friends stopped wanting to play. Her sister had married a young man from another village, and Belle hadn't heard from her since the day she left. She had a child now and another on the way. Belle was an aunt but would never see her niece.

All because the monster marked her.

Both her sister and she had been taken that winter night, but it was Belle that paid the price. Paid it in blood and tears and a broken heart.

She shook her head at her own melancholy and stepped out on the road. Today was her birthday. Her twenty-fourth. And while no one else was celebrating it, she was going to buy herself a new book. Reading had become her escape. A way of getting away from the village, the people, and the rumors.

The doors to the smithy were open, and she saw her father already hard at work, his young apprentice working the bellows.

She followed the road through the village and ignored the whispers around her. A mother, someone Belle had once called a friend, grabbed her child and crossed the street, making the sign of the cross in front of her chest. Belle blinked away the tears and kept going.

Don't let them see you cry, she told herself angrily.

She gave a relieved sigh when she ducked into the small store, the little bell over the door jingling at her arrival. She pushed the door closed behind her and

She hurried out to the main room and found her father looking at her with a scowl.

"Where is lunch?" he asked and looked around the kitchen.

Lunch? Oh no. "I'm sorry, papa. I'll get you something right now." She got some bread, cheese, and butter for him and a cup of the thin ale he favored. She couldn't believe she had lost time like that. Hours lost and not a single chore done.

Belle was exhausted when it was finally time for bed. She had been running herself ragged, trying to catch up, and still, she couldn't stop herself from sneaking in a page or two from her book. If only a handsome prince would come and take her away. She would even let him lock her up in a castle if it meant leaving this place.

You are losing your mind, my dear Belle, if you're willingly agreeing to be locked up by a monster. She scolded herself. She had always prided herself on having a good head. She didn't fall for pretty words and especially wouldn't do as someone told her just because of title or money. She had learned a long time ago that the only thing that mattered was how a person acted.

She eyed her bed, her tired body screaming for her to fall into it, but she still had a few hours left of her birthday, and she would be damned if she would celebrate them in her sad little bed.

She grabbed her cloak and swung it over her shoulders before carefully opening the window. She easily slipped out into the darkening summer night and followed the path through the garden, past the small hut where chickens, the pig, and the cow were locked up for the night, and out into the meadow. She hurried through the tall grass, knowing her father was fast asleep and still scared he would somehow spot her dark form running toward the forest. When she finally reached the forest edge, her heart was hammering wild in her chest. Freedom, it said with each beat.

Belle took down the hood and let the wind play with her long hair. She walked among the trees, listening to the evening sounds of the forest animals. She knew she shouldn't go out here, not alone, and especially not at night.

Wolves, wild boars, and sometimes even bears made their home in the forest, but Belle had already met the biggest monster and survived.

She made her way to the small forest lake. The water was still, reflecting the hues of the evening sky as the sun was swallowed by the horizon. She sat on the giant boulder where she had spent many nights and stared at the water, getting lost in her thoughts.

Beast steered his horse between the trees, following the little used path that would lead him a safe distance past the village. He had been here before, years ago. Hunting the same monster he had finally killed this day. For fifteen years, he had looked for it. Ten years of knowing it was out there, killing and creating more monsters to haunt his life.

That he would find the monster in the same place it had first eluded him was either a miracle or a curse. A miracle because the monster could have fled to where ever it wished. A curse because being back brought memories. Memories of two little scared girls. One blond and pretty with wet cheeks and dripping eyes. The other quiet and brave, with torn skin and bloody clothes. He had saved them, but in doing so, he had let the monster go.

He had given them both back to the town, but he had lingered for weeks, watching, waiting. Looking for the slightest hint of the girl turning. She had healed, showing a strength few men could match, and when he was sure no curse had befallen her, he had left and vowed to never return. But the monster had brought him back.

His horse shied under him, disturbed by something in the darkening forest. He stopped and listened, and heard it, faintly. A low whisper of a song, carried by the breeze.

He turned his horse and followed the song, and as he drew nearer, it pulled at him, calling him in. When he reached a small clearing, he spotted a figure sitting on a rock, back towards him. He jumped from the horse and tied it to a tree before walking closer. The song stopped, and the figure turned, gasping as she saw him so near.

"I'm sorry," he said and held his hands out. "I didn't mean to startle you."

The woman, her face hidden in the shadows of her hood, jumped from the rock and backed away. Not that he could blame her. Meeting strange men late at night was not something most maidens wished to try.

He was sure she would run without saying a word, but after a few steps back, she stopped. He felt her gaze even as her face was hidden in the hood of her cloak.

"It's… It's you," she said and took an unsure step closer.

"Have we met before?" he asked, trying to remember. To call forth something from all the memories clouding his mind.

"You're the lost prince." She laughed and stepped closer, reaching forward as if to touch his face, despite the distance between them.

"I think you're mistaken." He took a step back. All he had to do was get on his horse and ride away. Leave the area and not come back in this lifetime. In another eighty years, everyone who might remember anything would be dead.

"No, I'm not," the woman breathed out on a whisper and took the final steps to bring them close. She fell, her foot caught in something in the dark earth, and he grabbed her arm before she could hit the ground.

"Careful," he said and pulled her up, steadying her while she caught her footing. Her hood had fallen down, revealing a mass of dark hair trapped in a long braid. He starred into her dark eyes before she ripped herself out of his grip and covered her face with one hand as she tried to get the hood up with the other.

But he had already seen it. The long scar carving up her face. A long ragged slash from forehead to chin, twisting her left side. He grabbed her chin and turned her face, pulling her hand away so he could see it.

"You," he said and ran his fingers over the scar. It went straight through her eye, which was nothing but a milky white orb, and he wondered if her vision was impaired.

"Let go of me," she demanded of him and pulled her face out of his grasp, pushing him in the chest. Her fist connected with his cheek, and pain exploded in his head. He stumbled back, staring at the small woman in shock.

"How dare you? How dare you touch me?" The woman raised her hand again as if readying to hit him once more, thought better of it, and took a step back instead. "You left me. Left me to become an outcast, feared by everyone. I was the crazy one. The one saying she had seen the lost prince."

"I saved you," he said with a frown her way. He had done the right thing. Saved two little girls from the monsters. Maybe she was crazy. Not quite right in the head.

"Saved me? My own father looks at me with fear. My sister left town to get away from me and the rumors that haunt me. I would rather have died in that frozen cave than live this life." With those parting words, the small woman turned and ran between the trees.

Beast stared after her, too stunned to move. She hit him. Accused him of making her life hell after he saved her. Saving her probably cost lives as the monster had fifteen more years to go out hunting. And she was worried about a few rumors?

He wanted to go after her. Wanted to tell her just how an ungrateful little wench she was. But the hunt was still too fresh in his blood. He could already feel the blood pumping, hear his heart picking up speed. He breathed deeply, trying to calm down. She was just a woman. A silly woman from a small village, and she knew nothing about the world.

When he finally relaxed enough to unclench his jaw, he decided the forest lake was as good a place to set up his camp as any. He walked back to his horse, ignoring how he could still smell her in the air. It was just the battle rush talking. A good night's sleep and he would be ready to head home again.

Chapter 2

Belle ran, her breath burning in her lungs. She was so angry, more angry than she had ever been in her life. She had lost everything because he had just left her. When she had healed enough to get out of bed, she had been taken to the town's elders. Most of the town had been gathered in the town hall to hear the story about the monster. Her wounds had still been raw, half her body covered in bandages, but she had stood fast and told her tale. Told the truth. When she pointed at the painting of the lost prince, her father had grabbed her and told the elders that she was still confused. But Belle had insisted. The man who saved her might be older than the lost prince in the picture, but she was sure it was him.

She repeated her tale again and again until people started to whisper. At first, it was small things. That the trauma of the attack had left her mind fractured. That she just wanted attention. But then it grew.

She got in a fight with a boy that teased her sister, and suddenly the monster had infected her with its rage. She read and wrote better than some of the elders in town, and rumors started floating around that the monster had touched her with magic.

Then Gaston, the Miller's son, had tried to take liberties at the harvest festival. She wasn't sure why he had singled her out. Maybe he thought that she would be grateful or that no one would believe her. It didn't much matter why he had done it. She punched his nose, sending a spray of blood down his white shirt, and then she kicked him right between the legs as hard as she could. After that, Gaston had done everything in his power to make her life miserable, and she was sure half the rumors in town were caused by him.

Her hand throbbed from where she punched the rider. She wanted to curse herself. She knew how to punch. Had read it in books and even hidden in the shadows to watch the men box in the courtyard behind the villags only inn. But she had been so mad she had forgotten it all.

She paused at the edge of the garden and pulled in big gulps of air. Sweat covered her body, and she pulled her cloak off. It helped, but not enough. She was boiling from the inside. Stumbling to the still-open window, she crawled inside. In the darkness of her room, she pulled at her dress, unbinding the ties keeping it in place. Fabric ripped in her haste, and still, she burned. She sank to her knees, the cold stone floor feeling like a balm on her naked skin. She collapsed against the ground, pressing her forehead against the coldness. She couldn't think. Every thought burned away before it could take hold. All her scars tried to rip at the seams, the agony mixing with the flames eating her insides. Her nails dug into her skin. If only she could dig deep enough.

A glow moved on the other side of her door. Her father? She couldn't hear anything over the roar in her head. The light sharpened, and a single flame danced over the floor. She watched it, followed its path. It touched her outstretched hand, licking at her skin, matching the fire burning inside her.

The roar in her ears became deafening, and the fire inside her grew, feeding the little flame. It mixed, swirled, ripping her apart. She screamed and screamed, and not a single sound left her burning throat.

Beast woke to the smell of smoke heavy in the air. His head was a tangled mess, and he fought his blanket before he managed to sit up. A glow lighted between the trees towards the south. He frowned. They were hours from sunrise, and the sun did not rise on that path. He came to his feet and sniffed the air. Definitely something burning. Was the village on fire? He thought of the young woman. She had run that way. Was her home going up in flames?

He shook his head. He did not need to get involved in their lives. Getting involved only brought trouble and misery. He rolled up his blankets and secured them to his horse. If he rode out now, he would be long gone before morning came. He got on his horse and hesitated. Helping would be the right thing. No, he wasn't to get involved.

He followed the trail through the forest, but when the path split in two, he stopped again. With a growl at his own stupidity, he steered the horse left. He would just go close enough to get a quick look. Make sure the villagers had it all under control. Then he would be on his way.

At the edge of the forest, he got his first look at the flames. They ate through buildings at the edge of the village, flames rising to the heavens. Villagers were running back and forth. Someone screamed. He tied his horse to a tree and used the long grass in the meadow as cover as he moved closer. Just a single look, and then he would be on his way.

The last building, standing a little apart, was completely engulfed in flames. The roof was gone, the thatching long turned to ash. The wood groaned, and the structure collapsed. The roof beams fell with a sound like thunder, taking the walls with them.

A man fell to his knees, screaming. "Belle," the man shouted, again and again, agony in every word.

Beast had seen enough. The village would survive, even if sorrow would touch some. A shadow caught his eyes. Something moving inside the flames of the collapsed building. A trick of the eye, he was sure, but he kept his gaze fixed on the spot. Someone yelled, and more voices followed. The shadow moved again, and the air froze in his lungs. A monster? Here? Now?

Beast drew his blade. If the fire didn't take the monster, he would make sure to end it. His gaze tracked the shadowy form. It stirred again, rose up, and changed.

14

No, it couldn't be. She couldn't be one of the monsters. He had made sure of it. He had waited for weeks. Watched her every move. She had kept her human shape. Healed human slow. But it wasn't a monster stepping out of the flames, but a young woman. Belle. The firelight bathed her naked form and cast the old scars in shadows and light. Her hair had come undone and hung around her face and shoulders.

It wasn't possible. It should have burned. She should have burned. But not a blister showed. Not a single hair was singed.

How? If she was a monster, she would be trapped in that form. Forever caught in hell and rage.

Someone among the gathered people yelled witch, and more voices followed. The young woman was grabbed, her hand bound, and they pulled her away. Away from him.

He used the shadows, slipping from one spot to the next. The fire helped. No one was looking for strangers in the darkness when flames ate their homes. He followed the men who had taken her, watched as they tied her hands above her head to a pole marking the edge of a fence. She was naked and shivering, and he was close enough to see the tears running through the soot on her face.

They left then, back to the flames and fire. Just two men were left behind. One old enough to be a grandfather, the other young and strong. The older man looked at Belle, shook his head, and turned his back to her. A sob reached him, and he saw her folding in on herself. As if the last shreds of hope had been ripped from her body. The younger man was still staring at her, his gaze moving over her naked form.

He had to get her out of there. If she was one of the monsters, he had to stop her. She would have to die like the rest of them. But he had to be sure. Had to know what she was. They were monsters of ice and wind. Flames bit their skin and ate their flesh just as well as any other human.

Belle was shivering. The cold night air bit her body, but mostly it was fear that made her body shake. She stared at the flames eating her home and felt them call to her. She wanted to go to them, touch them. She swallowed and tried to fight the memories assaulting her. She had done this. She was the reason the village burned.

She looked at old Mr. Tobias, who stood with his back turned to her, and another sob broke loose. He had stood by her through everything. Always ready with a smile and a kind word, and now even he was lost to her.

Gaston took a step closer, leering at her naked body. She wished he was ugly and pockmarked. That the outside reflected the inside. But Gaston was the most handsome man in town. Handsome and strong, with the only thing marring his face the uneven form of his nose. She took great pride in knowing she was the cause of that imperfection.

"Maybe you should go home, Mr. Tobias. It's rather late, and you're an old man," Gaston said, his gaze never leaving Belle's body.

"I know my duty," Mr. Tobias said, his back still turned. "Perhaps you should remember yours."

Gaston's eyes darkened, and for a heartbeat, Belle feared Gaston would attack the old man. But then that slow charming smile the girls in the village always swooned over slid back in place.

"He won't stay awake all night," he whispered against her ear, his fingers pressing into her breast.

Fear tried to grab hold of her, but she pushed it down. He was a bully, and she would never show a bully her fear. She forced a smile, one she knew would be pulled into half a sneer because of the scar, and said loud enough for Mr. Tobias to hear, "I can't wait to break your nose one more time."

Gaston pulled back, anger twisting his pretty face, and slapped her. Blood filled her mouth, and she spit it on the ground, though she could feel some of it run down her chin.

She knew it was stupid to goad him when she stood naked and bound, but she didn't care. She had tried so hard to be good. Tried to keep her head down and not make trouble. And now they were going to burn her at the stake as a witch. Well, hell, take them all.

She opened her mouth to tell Gaston exactly what she thought about him, but the man suddenly turned away and walked to the well. She watched as he pulled the bucket up and drank from it, and she noticed how parched her own throat was. Another round of shivers raked her body, and her arms began to tingle from being bound above her head. The rope cut into her wrists, and even the tiniest movement made her feel like the rope cut deeper.

Fear wormed its way into her body, pushing into every corner of her mind. She didn't want to burn at the stake. She had seen it once when she was a little girl. She still remembered the screams and the stench of burning flesh and hair.

A wild thought hit her then. Could she burn? She had walked out of her burning home, not a single blister on her body. A crazy laugh bubbled out of her, ringing through the village. She laughed and laughed, unable to stop. It wasn't funny. It was completely, utterly horrifying. And still, she couldn't stop the laugh.

Gaston stalked over, and with a sneer on his face, he hit her square in the face.

Beast winced when Belle's crazy laugh rang out in the village. But the wince turned into a low growl when the young man hit her. Her head snapped back into the pole, and blood gushed out her nose, mixing with the blood already on her chin. He grabbed his sword tighter, but there was nothing he could do, not yet. Belle slumped in the ropes, and Beast cast a worried look at her hands. The rope they had used to bind her with was thin and rough, and if she was left for too long hanging like that, it would damage her hands.

Beast nearly cast aside all caution when the man's hands started roaming all over Belle's body. But before Beast could do something stupid, the old man barked out an order. The young man walked away, and the two of them settled down to wait. The old man was sitting on a barrel, leaning back against the wall of a house. The younger one was leaning against a post not far from Belle.

Beast took a chance and moved closer, as close as the shadows allowed. Belle was still breathing, her chest rising and falling in even slow movements. But even in the darkness of night, he could see her hands turning red, the weight of her body against the rope cutting off the blood flow. He glanced back at the two guards. The older one was nodding off, his eyes growing heavy.

Beast wouldn't get a better chance. The fire still roared behind him, keeping the villagers occupied, as he slowly rose from his hiding place. It wasn't hard to sneak up on the young man, and a hard blow to the back of his neck sent him limp to the ground. It burned in him to cut the man's throat. Beast was no saint, but he hated a man who took what he had no right to take. And there was no doubt in Beast's mind. The man would take whatever he wanted. He shook his head. Hurting the young man would cause trouble Beast didn't need. Taking the woman was already risky enough.

He quickly cut the bindings on Belle, catching her as she collapsed. It had only been half an hour, but her skin was ice to his touch. Her eyes didn't open as he swung her over his shoulder. He turned and found the old man watching him.

"Go, hurry, before they realize she's gone," the man whispered. Beast stared at him for a second before giving him a nod in thanks. He turned and made his way through the shadows, praying that the villagers wouldn't see him. Skies had covered the moon, making his escape less risky, and he managed to get to the forest without being seen.

He would take her home with him, and then he would solve this mystery.

Chapter 3

Belle blinked against the harsh light of day. Her mind was a jumbled mess, and she wasn't sure what was a dream and what was reality. She snuggled deeper into the blanket, the warmth like a safe little cocoon around her, protecting her from the harsh reality of life. She tried to make sense of her thoughts, but it was all such a mess. Had her home really burned? The faint smell of smoke clinging to her hair told her that that memory at least had to be true. Her nose hurt, and she carefully touched it with a finger. Had Gaston really hit her? She sat up with a gasp, air trapped in her lungs, and she looked around in fear. They had wanted to burn her at the stake, hadn't they?

She took in her surroundings, confusion mixing with her fear. She wasn't in the village. In fact, she had no idea where she was. It looked like a small forest clearing. The remnants of a fire marred the moss-covered ground beside her. Tall trees swayed gently in the wind, and she could hear birds and insects around her. She looked behind her and saw a big dark brown horse nipping at a small tuft of grass.

She had never seen a horse that big. It was easily taller than her, and hair covered its hooves. She absently noticed that three of the legs were white while one was so dark brown it was nearly black. But her attention was drawn to the side of the horse because there stood the lost prince. She stared at him like a startled deer. She wasn't sure if she had dreamed him up or if she had really met him in the woods. Everything in her mind was a confusing mess. But here he was. Flesh and blood.

As if he knew she was looking at him, he turned, and his eyes lighted a bit when a smile tucked at his lips.

"You're awake," he said.

Belle just stared at him. He had saved her. Again. *If it wasn't for him, you wouldn't be in this situation to begin with,* a small voice whispered in the back of her mind, and she clung to it, letting it fuel the tiny flame of her anger. It didn't matter if her rage was wrong or misplaced. Anything was better than the confusing mess she felt like.

She turned to follow him with her gaze as he moved towards her, and she felt clothes against her skin under the blankets. Had he dressed her? Heat rose in her cheeks. It was silly, but somehow it felt more intimate to know this man had dressed her than when the whole village had seen her naked.

He crouched by the burned-down fire and picked up a small pot. He stirred it, and the scent of herbs hit her. Her stomach cramped, and she realized she was ravenous.

"Here, try taking a few sips." He handed her a small

cup, and she carefully took a mouthful, keenly aware that he was following every move.

The soup was lukewarm, and some kind of strange herb almost bit her tongue, and still, it was the most delicious thing she had ever tasted. She greedily drank it all down, despite his warning about taking it slow, but she was so hungry. He frowned at her but handed her a flask of water. She tipped the flask, letting the cool water soothe her throat.

"You'll make yourself sick," the lost prince said and snatched the flask away from her. She glared at him, but in truth, her stomach was cramping a bit.

He sat down on the other side of the fire and looked at her with hard eyes. "What happened?" he asked.

Even if her head hadn't been a jumbled mess, she had learned her lesson all those years ago. So instead of answering him, she just shook her head. There was no way she would tell this stranger about the fire dancing towards her or the anger and fear. About how she had boiled from the inside and walked through the flames without a single mark on her body.

"Look, I can't help if I don't know what happened."

"Who are you?" she asks instead. She had been staring at the ground, but now she sneaked a small glance at him. He was looking at her intently, a small frown pulling at his lips. She had never seen anyone with eyes like his. One was a clear blue and the other a golden that almost shone in the sunlight. Even clouded with annoyance and maybe anger from her refusal to answer, they were the prettiest eyes she had ever seen.

"I'm Beast."

She stared at her openly, her mouth open, before

she burst out laughing. "Beast?" No one was named beast, especially not someone like him. Sure he was big and strong. Bigger than most in the village, but that hardly made him a beast. She thought back to the soldiers that had passed through the village a few years back. One of the soldiers had been a mountain of a man. Long shaggy hair and a beard hiding most of his face. That man had been a beast.

Beast frowned at the woman. He had thought she might not be quite right in her head when he met her in the forest, and now he was sure of it. What kind of woman laughed at a man who had her alone in the woods?

"I don't see why my name is so funny," he grumbled and got to his feet. He had to pack up the last of the things, so they could be on their way.

"Your mother didn't name you beast," she said and arched her eyebrow over the good eye.

"I don't remember what my mother named me. Beast is the name my fellow soldiers gave me, and I have taken it as my own."

Belle opened her mouth, closed it again, and looked down at the ground. "I'm sorry. My name is Belle."

"I know," he said. He held out his hand, and she stared at it with distrust.

"I need the blanket so we can be on our way."

"Where are we going?" she asked and handed over

24

the blanket. She looked down at herself and gasped. She did look rather silly dressed in his shirt and pants. Both billowed around her tiny frame, making her look like a small child playing dress up. But silly was better than naked. Much better. Her naked body brought all kinds of sinful thoughts. Thoughts he had long ago pushed away from his life.

"I'm taking you to my home."

"Why?" she frowned at him, mistrust clear in her single brown eye.

He didn't answer her, not willing to voice his suspicions. If he was wrong and she wasn't a monster, there was no reason to fill her head with those ideas. He looked at her scared face and remembered the rest of the scars marring her body. She already knew there were monsters in the world. No reason to make her believe she was one of them, too.

Belle backed away from him, her eyes narrowing in anger. "I'm not going anywhere with you."

"Don't be silly. You have nowhere to go, no money, and no provisions," he said and strode over to her. He grabbed her arm, intent on bringing her back to his horse. They wouldn't be safe before they got to his home, and he didn't like the slow pace he'd been forced to travel with her so far. They needed to put more distance between themselves and the village.

He barely avoided the fist swinging at him. "Don't," he said and grabbed her hand when she made another attempt. He had to give it to her; she was a feisty one.

"I want to know why we are going to your home." She glared up at him, anger burning in her eyes, and he couldn't help but smile.

"It's not funny," she said and tried to pull away.

"You're right. I apologize." He looked into her eyes. "I'm taking you to my home because you can be safe there." And the world could be safe from her, but he didn't add that part.

Belle frowned but then gave a slow nod. Good, she saw reason, at least.

He indicated the horse, and Belle stared at him with wide eyes. "You want me to ride on that?"

"His name is Agathon, and no, you are not riding him. We are." He grabbed Belle around the waist and swung her up on the horse. She was a very small thing, and he was a lot stronger than he looked. She gave a girlish scream and clutched the saddle as he swung up behind her. It was a tight fit, the saddle was definitely not designed for two riders, but it would have to do. He nudged Agathon, and the horse happily set off through the trees. He wanted to go home too.

Belle was acutely aware of the man behind her. At first, she had been sitting stiffly, trying to keep as much distance between them as possible, but the gentle movements of the horse lulled her exhausted brain into a place where she just didn't care, and she leaned back against Beast, trusting him to keep her from falling.

Her mind was finally catching up to the events that

had transpired. Meeting him in the forest, the strange anger, the fire. She remembered Gaston's lusty gaze and suppressed a shudder. Had he taken any liberties after he knocked her out? She didn't think so, but the thought alone made her sick to her stomach.

"Are you unwell?" Beast's rumbling voice asked.

"No, I'm fine, thank you." She swallowed the bile rising at those thoughts and concentrated on Agathon instead. She ran her hands over the soft fur on his neck and twirled a few strands of his long mane through her fingers. She had never ridden a horse before, and she found she rather enjoyed the experience. She had been around horses before, of course. The village had a few workhorses used in the fields and used to pull the wagons. And travelers with their wagons and riders came through once in a while, but she had always found the animals to be a bit scary. And none of them had been as massive as Agathon.

She had much preferred being around Dottie, the small cow her father owned. Tears unwittingly sprang to her eyes as she thought of the animals locked up for the night. Had they burned to death in the fire?

"Hey, are you crying?" A strong hand grabbed her face, and her head was turned. She blinked and looked into Beast's worried eyes.

"What's wrong?" he asked, wiping a few tears from her face.

"It's stupid."

"Tell me anyway."

"I just realized that the fire might have killed all the animals." Saying it out loud made her feel even worse.

Beast pulled on the rains, and Agathon dutifully

stopped moving. Beast didn't say anything. He just wrapped her up in his arms and pulled her close. She tried to fight it, but in the end, she buried her face in his chest and cried. Big ugly sobs that shook her whole body. She cried because she might never see her father again. She cried for the home she had lost. But mostly, she cried for sweet Dottie, who loved carrots and getting her head scratched. She didn't notice when they started moving again or when she dosed off, held close to Beast's chest.

When she woke again, the sky had turned a deep orange and purple, and darkness was creeping in between the trees. She rubbed her eyes. They felt like someone had filled them with sand, and she was sure she looked all puffy and red. Not that it mattered. Her scar made sure she would never be pretty, and out here in the forest, with only Beast around, who would care?

The tenderness he had shown her when she cried seemed to have vanished with the sun. He sat stiffly behind her, and when he stopped Agathon and jumped to the ground, he didn't as much as look her way. Not that she blamed him. Having a woman he hardly knew sob against his chest, only for her to then fall asleep against him, was probably not what most men wanted. She carefully slung her leg over the back of Agathon, glad she wore pants and not a skirt, and slid to the ground. Her butt hurt, and her legs felt wobbly enough that she kept a tight grip on the saddle, hoping Agathon wouldn't mind.

When it felt like she could stand on her own, she turned only to find the forest empty. She turned in a circle and even walked to the other side of Agathon, but there was no trace of Beast.

"Your master is a strange man," she said to the horse and hugged herself a bit. She was a stranger, but he wouldn't leave his horse, would he?

Get it together, Belle. Why would he take you all the way out here just to leave you? She told herself sternly. Most likely, he had walked away to relieve himself.

Deciding that she at least could be a little useful, she grabbed the reins of Agathon and tied him to a tree before setting out to collect wood for a fire.

When Beast returned, carrying a fat goose in one hand, Belle had a fire going and was trying to figure out how to get the saddle off Agathon. She had loosened the strap under his belly, but when she tried to slide it off the big animal, the saddle nearly hit her in the head, and she frantically pushed it back in place only for it to try and slip off the other side. She was pretty sure it would be bad if the saddle hit the ground from that height, and after stabilizing it back on the horse, she had set out to find a solution to the problem.

She glanced at Beast. The easiest solution would be for him to lift it off, but the sour look on his face kept her from asking. Besides, how hard could it be? There had to be some trick to it that would let her get it off safely. She contemplated pulling Agathon over to a fallen tree and using it to stand on. If she got up higher, she would have no problem lifting the damn thing. The whole issue was only there because Agathon was so tall.

"You've been staring at my horse for a quarter of an hour. I hope you aren't thinking about stealing him." There was no teasing in those words, and it made Belle's hackles rise.

"I'm not a thief," she snapped back, but she didn't look away from the horse.

With a sigh, Beast stepped over and stood beside her, looking at the horse too. Then, as if it was the easiest thing in the world, he grabbed the saddle and pulled it off.

Belle glared at him, the urge to try and hit him again burning through her. She was so close to finding a solution, and he just took over? He rummaged through one of the saddlebags and pulled out a stiff brush.

"Brush him down while I get the goose cooking." He handed her the brush and walked back to the fire, leaving her glaring after him. She wanted to throw the brush on the ground and stalk off. Or even better, throw it at his head.

"Don't even think about throwing that at me," Beast said and gave her a pointed stare. Belle grabbed the brush harder. His words only fueled her anger, and the urge to do it just because he said she shouldn't, was overwhelming. She wasn't a child, and he had no right to order her around or talk to her like that. Heat burned in her chest as she stared daggers at Beast. He was leaning over the fire, spreading out the coals and adding more wood. The anger and heat snapped in her chest, and the fire suddenly flared up. Beast fell back, shielding his face.

Belle gasped and briefly met Beast's shocked face before turning to Agathon. Had she done that? With shaking hands, she started to brush the horse. It wasn't

Agathon's fault his master was a cur. Dust and hair whirled around her, and Agathon sighed with pure horse happiness. She took longer than needed to brush out the horse, but she wasn't ready to face Beast. The anger and fire in her were completely gone, but it had felt familiar. As if it was a lesser version of what happened the night her father's house burned. But that couldn't be true. She wasn't a witch, was she? No. She had never prayed to the devil or done anything evil. So then what? Was it all just a coincidence?

Beast cleaned the goose quickly and put it over the fire. He knew he had been wrong in leaving her as he had, but he had needed to get away. To be able to breathe and think without her body pressed against his. Despite everything not adding up, the likelihood of her being a monster was high, and he couldn't afford to become attached to her company. No, he just had to figure out what she was, and then he would either end her life or let her go. The skin on his face felt tight, and he wasn't sure what had made the flames flare up like that. He glanced at Belle. Had she caused it? Or had he been too focused on her and not paid attention to the fire?

He turned the goose and watched her brush Agathon. His big stallion didn't seem to mind the attention and happily rubbed his head against her side, begging for a treat or a good scratch. She giggled at his antics and gave him the sought-after scratch.

He didn't understand it. He had stayed all those years and watched her, and she had shown no sign of changing. But he couldn't deny she had walked out of that fire without a single mark. But the monsters were creatures of ice and snow. And once they got infected, they lost all trace of humanity. Becoming raving beasts who hunted anything that might make a good meal. But if she wasn't a monster, then what? A witch? His lip rose in a silent snarl at the thought. Witches were worse than any monster. A monster would kill you. A witch would curse you forever. Bringing only misery and loneliness into existence. Could she be a witch? He tried to think back, but he had no memories of her mother.

But in reality, the likelihood of her being a witch was smaller than her being a monster. Except she was standing there, as human as himself. So what, then?

The only other thing he could think of was if she was like him. But that wasn't possible. Was it? He had been cursed, and had wandered the earth for hundreds of years. How could she be like him?

He shook his head. It was all guesswork. He needed to bring her to the castle, and then he'd figure it out. When the full moon came, he would know if she truly was a monster. He looked at the sky. They still had fourteen days. They would reach his castle in four if all went as it should. Fourteen days, and he'd have his answers.

Chapter 4

Belle woke with a start, fear skittering around in her mind.

Just a dream. It was just a dream. She ran a hand through her tangled hair. Maybe she should use Agathon's brush to try and untangle it. Beast was lightly snoring, the morning light playing over his face. She had to admit he was a very handsome man. Not the way Gaston was handsome, with his thick wavy hair and high cheekbones. No, Beast was handsome in a rugged kind of way. His hair was long and just as tangled as hers, if not more. He had worn it tied back all day yesterday, but now it was a knotted mess all around his face. A beard covered his face, but it was trimmed rather short, and she expected that when he was home, it would be kept neatly. A small scar covered his right cheek just above the beard, and another split his eyebrow in two. She touched her own scar. It ran through her left eyebrow and eye, across her cheek, through her lips, and ended on the right side of her chin. The loss of her vision had been the worst. No one knew why her eye had turned white, but her sight was gone in that eye. It had taken her months and months to learn to navigate again. She had kept walking into things.

She looked back at Beast. He wanted to take her back to his home, where ever that was, but she had no intention of going with him.

She still remembered the night she had been taken by the monster, despite wishing so many times that she didn't. She remembered the anger on Beast's face, and the hatred in his eyes, that had almost been glowing with it. He was a dangerous man, and he was lying to her. She was sure of it. He said she needed to come with him because it was dangerous for her on her own. And she was just to believe that he was doing it out of the goodness of his heart when he seemed to wish her far away half the time?

No, she would be better off on her own. She just had to find the right time to get away from him because she had a distinct feeling that if she was to get up and walk away right this second, he would drag her right back.

Beast stirred and blinked open his startling eyes. She looked away and sat up, trying to form a plan. Her gaze landed on the leftovers from last night's dinner. He had managed to kill a goose, which meant there most likely was water nearby.

"Is there a lake near us?" she asked while gathering her blankets. The morning air was warm, and not a wind stirred. She looked up at the sky. Not a single cloud. It would be another burning hot day, it seemed.

"Yes, maybe five minutes that way." He pointed over his shoulder and got up himself. He started to pack up the blankets, and Belle tried to formulate a quick plan. A five minutes head start wasn't much, but then, if she walked to the lake alone, it would be at least a quarter of an hour before he came looking for her.

"Would you mind if I go and wash up a bit? I still smell of the fire, and I feel rather dirty." She carefully avoided looking at him, afraid he would see her intentions in her eyes. Instead, she busied herself with folding her blankets and rolling them carefully.

"I guess we can have a slow start this morning," Beast said, but she caught the hesitation in his voice. Grabbing hold of that, she asked, her voice a tiny pitch higher, "do you think they are following us?"

"Oh, no, I don't believe they are."

"Goody, then I'll just be off then." Blanket in hand, she strode through the forest. Her feet were bare, but the ground was covered in moss and soft grasses, and she didn't mind feeling the earth beneath her. She just hoped it wouldn't hinder her too much when she had to run. She walked for a few minutes, looking over her shoulder as often as possible to see if he followed. When she was sure he wasn't, she threw the blanket on the ground and ran.

She had no idea where it was safe to go, but everywhere would be better. A mountain peak rose on the horizon, and she used it as her mark. As long as she ran towards that, she would hopefully hit a road at some point. She just had to keep a straight line, or she would end up lost forever in this forest.

Her legs burned, the soles of her feet were raw, and

35

it was a chore to pull in air to fill her lungs when she suddenly stumbled from the forest and hit a road. It was a well-used road because it was mostly free of weeds and grass, and Belle's hopes soared. A well-traveled road meant there had to be a big town at each end. She looked both ways, and her heart almost stopped when she saw a figure step from the forest. How had he found her so fast? But it wasn't Beast. In fact, it was an old woman carrying a basket. Belle ran a hand through her hair, trying to dislodge the twigs and leaves that had gotten stuck in her mad run, and walked over to the woman.

"Hello," she said carefully, keeping her distance, so she didn't scare the woman. The woman looked up at her and gave her an almost toothless smile.

"Ello, child."

"Do you know where the nearest town is?" It couldn't be too far away if an old woman was wandering this road.

"The nearest town is five hours that way." She pointed down the road, and Belle almost gave a deep sigh. Her feet already hurt so much, and she wasn't sure how she would manage walking for six hours. Besides, walking for that long gave Beast a lot of opportunities to catch her.

The old woman looked down and gasped loudly when she saw Belle's bare feet. "Oh, child, what have you been doing? Come, come." She grabbed Belle's arm and pulled her down the road. Belle reluctantly followed, but how dangerous could an old lady really be?

They walked around a bend in the road, and Belle

stopped when she saw the three wagons pulled by oxen. The wagons were painted in bright green, and cloths, ropes, and bells hung on the outsides. Children ran around playing, and men and women walked beside the wagons, probably making sure the oxen didn't have that extra burden.

The old woman gave a small push, and Belle walked closer. It wasn't hard to catch up to the wagons. It seemed no one was in a hurry to get where they were going. But maybe they weren't going anywhere. They were travelers. She had only seen them a few times and always from a distance. They weren't welcome in her little village, and they always took the road that went past it instead of through.

The old woman waved a man over. "I am Marie, and this is my son, Phillipe."

"Belle," she said and tried not to hide her face as she felt the man look at her scars.

"Phillipe, stop staring. Go find Nicolas' old boots." She swatted the man's arm, and he dutifully turned around to do as told.

"Nicolas is my grandson. He grows like the weeds, and I think his old boots will be about your size." The old woman still had a strong hold on her arm and pulled Belle with her toward the nearest wagon. Belle thought about protesting, but if these people could help her, she would be in a much better place.

37

Beast had packed up camp and ensured the fire was completely out, and Belle still hadn't returned. He looked up at the sky and decided she had had enough time to wash up. Grabbing Agathon's rains, he led the horse into the forest towards the small lake.

He didn't go far before he spotted the blanket on the ground. His heart skipped a beat. Had she been taken? No, she couldn't have. There was no one out here.

He stood with the blanket in his hand and realized she had run. He had been so sure she saw that she had no other choice than to follow him that he never thought she would try to run. Clearly, he had been a fool. He swung up on Agathon, but which way had she run? He would never find her if he chased her in the wrong direction. He rode in circles, slowly widening his search area until he finally found a clear print in the bare earth between the moss and grass. He looked up and spotted the mountain in the distance. If she kept that as her mark, he had a chance to find her. He put his heels to Agathon, and the big horse shot forth.

When he finally reached the road, he was cursing and pulling twigs from his hair. Agathon was not made for mad dashes through the forest. Beast looked up and down the road. She could have taken both ways. He tried to place his position in his mind. If he was correct, there was a town only some hours away if he went to the right. If he took the left road, he would have a two-day trip. Having nothing to go on, he turned Agathon to the right. Hopefully, they would find Belle fast.

Half an hour later, he found signs that wagons had

passed through not long ago. His hopes fell. If Belle had passed through here, there was a chance someone had picked her up. Either they had already captured her and were willing to hand her over as a witch, or they were kind people who would help her. Getting her back had just become increasingly harder.

With a curse, he let Agathon set the pace. There was no reason in tiring the horse when a faster pace wouldn't help.

How could she be so stupid? Didn't she realize that the word about the witch would have spread by now? And with her scar, she was easy enough to pick out of the crowd, even by a stranger. A sudden realization hit him. She didn't know. She had been slipping in and out of fever for three days before she woke up, and she didn't remember.

In her mind, it had only been a day since he rescued her, not four. He swore loudly and asked Agathon to pick up his speed, and the big horse easily complied.

"You are a rather small thing, aren't you?" Marie looked Belle up and down, pulling at the men's clothing she wore.

Belle bit her tongue not to laugh. Marie was almost half a head smaller than her.

"I think you might be able to fit my Emilie's clothes." Marie wrapped a rope around Belle's waist and nodded to herself. "It will be too long in the skirts, but none in my family is as small as you."

"I'm not that small," Belle said and crossed her arms over her chest, glaring at the old woman. She knew she was small. She had been the smallest woman in her village. Her mother had been a tall woman, and her father was among the tallest in town, so Belle had no idea why she wasn't bigger. Her little sister had grown above her head when Belle was fourteen and her sister twelve. Maybe it was because of her wounds, or maybe she had just been unlucky.

Marie just laughed at her. "You are the definition of petite. I think most would mistake you for a child if it weren't for those shapes." She indicated Belle's breasts and hips.

Belle just sighed and stripped out of her clothes. Marie had found her a smock, a skirt, and a vest. It was dyed in a pretty blue, and even faded as the color was, Belle had never worn anything as pretty. There was a knock on the door, and then Phillipe stuck his head inside. He smiled at her before placing a pair of boots on the floor and jumping down again from the moving wagon.

"He will never grow up, that one. You would not think he is married and has three living children." Marie shook her head and grabbed a brush. "Now, you sit down, and I'll help with this hair."

Chapter 5

"Thank you so much." Belle leaned down and hugged Marie before turning to face the town gate. The travelers would set up their wagons outside the town, but Belle was going inside. Hopefully, she could find something, anything, that could help her. The town was surrounded by a wall, but the gates were open wide, and people were walking freely in and out. She had never seen so many people or a town this big.

Pulling her new cloak around her, making sure the hood covered her face, she made her way inside the wall. The throng of people almost carried her through the streets, and she tried to take in everything she saw. Buildings rose up on either side of her. She had never seen anything other than the one-story buildings in her village, but she had read about them, and seeing them in real life was fantastical. Her heart beat with happiness when she realized she had made it. She was actually free. Free from her past, free from the rumors. Free from the village.

A market was going on at the town square, and Belle felt overwhelmed by the sounds, smells, and sights that met her. Stalls formed narrow pathways, and she walked among them, looking at everything they sold. Colorful fabrics, fruits and vegetables she didn't have a name for, and more food than she had ever seen. Her stomach rumbled, but she had no money to buy anything with.

She needed to find herself a job. Marie had told her that the town had more than a few taverns and inns. Belle's hope was to find a job in one of them. She had been running her father's house ever since her mother died, and she was a hard worker.

She stopped by a stall selling books, her mind not quite believing what she saw. She had always thought old Mr. Tobias had quite a big collection, but compared to this stall, his collection was nothing. The stall was actually a wagon, much like the travelers used. Except this one was missing one side, and shelves filled every inch of the inside. Books of all colors and sizes greeted her where ever she looked. A man stood in front of the wagon, a long table in front of him piled high with even more books.

It itched in her hands to grab them, but instead, she tugged her hands inside her cloak and turned to leave. She almost cursed when someone bumped into her, ripping her hood off her head. She hurried to pull it back up, looking around to see if anyone had spotted her, but everyone just kept going, not even sparing her a glance.

Belle looked around and spotted what looked to be the main street out of the town center. If she was to find a tavern, that was probably the place to start looking. She made her way to the edge of the market. There were so many people that it would be impossible to easily make it across the center, so following the edge seemed to be the fastest option.

She walked past a darkened alley, running down between two tall buildings when someone grabbed her arm and pulled her into the shadows. A hand was clasped over her mouth and nose, and she struggled to draw in air. Desperate for a breath, she yanked her head to the side and bit as hard as she could into her attacker's hand. A man howled behind her, and she tasted blood on her tongue when he ripped his hand away. Belle spit out the blood and flesh, ready to scream. A hand wrapped around her throat, and she was slammed against the wall. A fist hit her head, and she blinked away the tears that filled her eyes as pain exploded in her mind. More blood filled her mouth, and the inside of her cheek throbbed where her teeth had ripped her open.

She finally saw her two attackers. They were both in their mid-twenties, and their clothing was shabby but clean. One was a bit taller than the other, and the one holding her throat, slowly choking her to death, was fair-haired to the other man's darker curls.

She wasn't quite sure why she was noticing these things instead of fighting for her life.

"Are you sure it's her?" the taller one asked. The one she had bit.

"How many witches do you know walking around with scars like that?" the fair-haired one nodded toward Belle's face. The man grinned at her, showing yellow teeth and a gap where there used to be a front tooth.

"Now, keep your mouth shut, you little witch, or I'll cut out your tongue. No one cares if a witch can talk or not when she's getting hanged."

How did they know? Belle froze with fear. Her mind reeling with the fact they knew who she was. They were far from her little village, she was sure of it.

The man loosened his grip and let go of her, and she dragged in a full lungful of air. The more air she pulled into her starving lungs, the more reason returned. It didn't matter how they knew. All that mattered was how she got out of this town before anyone else spotted her.

She spat out blood and glared at the men. She had to run. It was her only chance.

The men pushed her down the alley, and she stumbled across the slick cobblestone, the stench of piss and old ale permeating the air.

There was a small opening between two houses at the end of the alley. If she could get to it, she could squeeze through. The two men holding her were too big. She took a chance and ran. The man she had bitten grabbed for her, and his fingers snagged on the end of her braid. She stumbled and felt fingers close around her arm, so tight it felt like her bone might break.

"Stupid bitch," the man said. He pushed her, and she stumbled into the wall, her scared side slamming into it, making little spots dance in her vision on her good side. For a second, she thought something moved in the shadows, but before she could be sure, she was pulled upright and dragged further down the alley.

Stupid, Belle. You should have waited, she berated herself. Now she had to hope another opportunity would present itself.

Something growled. The sound rolled down the

alley, and fear skirted down Belle's back. She had heard that sound before. The day the lost prince had saved her from the monster.

Beast stepped out of the shadow, looking at the two men with murder in his eyes.

"Let her go," he growled. Both men released Belle and stepped back as if they would get burned if they didn't. They wouldn't get burned, but it might hurt just the same.

He focused on Belle. Her body shook, and tears ran down her cheeks, mixing with the blood that marred her chin. Anger burned in her eye, though he didn't miss the flashes of fear. She swayed lightly on her feet, and worry shot through him. Had she hit her head hard enough to do damage? Beast stopped in front of her, making sure she was focused on him, that she knew it was him, before he reached up and wiped the tears from her face.

"It's okay, I'm here now," he whispered to her. She slowly nodded but winced when his thumb swiped over a mark on her cheek. He grabbed her chin and turned her face enough to catch the sparse light. A bruise was forming on her cheek under a few superficial scratches. His eyes quickly took it all in,

45

and then he noticed the red marks on her throat.

Rage burned through him, fast and swift. They had choked her.

"Who did this to you?" He almost growled the words and swallowed deeply a few times to keep from scaring her. He released her face when she didn't answer him. She was by far the most stubborn woman he had ever met. Instead, he turned to the two men, who didn't seem to have much survival instincts in their bodies because instead of running, they both stood with their backs against the wall.

Or maybe they were smart and realized that running from a predator just made the hunt so much sweeter.

"Which one of you two did this to her? Which one of you dared touch her?" he stalked closer, looking each man over. Their clothes had seen better days, and both of them looked like they could use an extra meal or two, which didn't bode well for them when winter hit and food got harder to get.

None of the men said a word.

"If none of you will talk, I'll just assume it was you both and take a hand from each of you."

The tallest one took a step away and pointed to the smallest of the two. Beast grabbed the smaller man around the throat and slammed him into the wall. He was of a mind to just keep on slamming him until the man's head cracked like an egg.

"Did you touch her?"

The man nodded, his face slowly turning red. Beast leaned in close enough to whisper in the man's ear so Belle wouldn't hear. "No one touches what is mine." He had no idea where the words came from, but seeing

46

her hurt like that had his beast howling for blood and his human half wanting to cut them into little pieces.

Beast grabbed a knife from his belt but hesitated. Belle was the one who had been wronged.

"Do you want them dead?" Beast wouldn't lose a single minute of sleep if these two men died, but Belle might.

"Excuse me?" she narrowed her eyes at him.

"They hurt you. They were going to give you over to torture and hanging. So you get to decide. Do they live or die?"

Belle opened her mouth, closed it again, and frowned. Beast nearly laughed. She was actually thinking it over.

"Let them live," she finally said. And then she surprised him by walking up to him and stating, "but make sure they never forget this." Then she turned and walked towards the end of the alley, further away from the town center.

"Please, don't," the smallest man forced out, his face taking on an unhealthy color. Beast ignored his pleading and let go of his throat. The man nearly doubled over, sucking in air. Beast grabbed his hand instead, pressed it against the wall, and before the man had air enough in his lungs to say a single word, Beast slammed the knife through the hand and into the rough wooden beam of the building. The man gasped, too stunned to even scream. Beast turned his back to him and caught the other man, who had finally decided it would be in his best interest to run.

It was more of a struggle to get the second man over to the beam, but Beast was taller and stronger,

47

and if anyone heard the man yelling, they chose to ignore it.

When both men were nailed to the beam, Beast looked them both over.

"Just remember, you live because she thought your lives worth saving." He grabbed another knife from his belt and sliced both men across their faces, leaving a bleeding gash as a visual reminder. He gave them both a disgusted look, turned, and caught up with Belle.

"Come, I know the way out, and Agathon is waiting for us." Belle didn't argue as he led them through the back streets to a smaller gate in the wall. He quickly got Belle on the horse and made sure her hood was covering everything before he spurred Agathon and rode as fast as the horse could run away from the town.

When he finally felt they were at a safe distance, he went off the road and made his way through the trees. If they were lucky, the men would keep their mouths shut, but more than likely, they were already telling their story to the city guards.

"Why did you run?" he finally asked Belle, but the furiously irritating woman didn't answer, just shook her head and stared down at her hands.

Belle was equally scared and furious.

Scared because she was sure Beast was one of the monsters. She had had her suspicion. Memories from the night the monster took her. Of his hands turning into claws and his eyes glowing, but she had always just thought it was her mind being confused because how could a man be one of those monsters? But that growl, she remembered that growl. The way it made every fiber in her body scream that something dangerous was near. She had heard it the day she and her sister had been taken, and she never thought she would hear it again. But she had, and it had come from Beast.

And she was furious because this was the third time he had saved her, and each time her life somehow became worse than it was. He saved her, and she became an outcast. He saved her, and she became hunted as a witch. Now he had saved her again, and she was his prisoner. He hadn't said as much, but Belle understood the writing on the wall. Alone, she was hunted and risked death. The only chance she had, was going with him.

They rode until night, and the silence between them was deafening. When Beast finally stopped to make camp, her body was sore and cramping. Her feet hurt in the boots, and her legs told her she had run too much. Coupled with the unfamiliarity of riding, she was ready to collapse as soon as her feet hit the ground. Beast didn't go out to hunt, and they didn't start a fire. He just pulled some dried meat from one of the saddle packs, and Belle forced herself to chew through the tough meat before she wrapped the blanket around her and let sleep drag her under.

Flames licked up her body, almost blinding her as she stared out at the gathered people. Her father, her sister, old Mr. Tobias, Gaston, and all the people she had known her whole life stood watching her as the flames consumed her. She tried to get free, but her hands were tied. She stared at her father and screamed his name, but he just turned his head away. She saw his lips move, and she shouldn't have been able to hear his words through the fire, but she did. "Thank god she's gone. Let her be the devil's burden now."

"No," she screamed, but the fire blinded her vision, licking up her body like soft caresses, and then they grew firmer, hands against her naked skin. Groping and pulling. She couldn't see anything, but somewhere behind the groping hands and the blindness, she heard the frightened screams of Dottie burning to death.

"Belle, wake up, dammit, it's just a dream."

Belle jerked upright, fear clawing at her. She was blind. She couldn't see.

"Easy, it's the middle of the night. Take a few deep breaths."

She did as told, and slowly her vision came back. Beast was kneeling next to her, looking at her with worry.

"It was just a dream," she whispered. Her voice was raw and scratchy.

"Nightmare, more like it. You were screaming and fighting your blanket." He handed her a flask with water, and she greedily drank from it. The cool water soothed her throat.

"I'm sorry for waking you up."

"Don't be. We don't control the things we see in our dreams." He sounded like he talked from experience, and maybe he did. He did say he had gotten his name as a soldier. He probably had his fair share of bad memories.

"Let's get back to sleep," he said.

Belle nodded, but she knew there would be no sleep for her. The dream had been too real. She could still hear Dottie's screams ring in her ears. Or maybe it was her own.

"Belle?"

She looked over to where Beast was sitting on his blanket. Since they didn't have a fire, their bedding was much closer than normal. If she reached out, she would be able to touch him.

"Yeah?" she whispered back. The night was so quiet, and it felt wrong, somehow, to speak any louder.

He didn't say anything, just grabbed his blanket and moved it closer to hers. She wanted to protest. It wasn't right for them to sleep so close together, but she didn't say a word. She had crossed the bridge away from "proper" a long time ago.

Beast pulled her down into his arms and wrapped her blanket over them. It felt weird to sleep so close to another person. Especially this person. She ought to be scared of him, but she wasn't. For all that had happened in her life, Beast hadn't hurt her. That didn't mean he was blameless or that she liked him. In fact, she hated him with every fiber in her body. Somehow he was tied to every bad thing that ever happened in

51

her life. And even if it was illogical, she couldn't help but place the blame on him. But hatred or not, she felt safe wrapped in his arms. And maybe she hated him for that too.

She snuggled closer to his chest and breathed deeply. And somehow, sleep found her anyway.

Chapter 6

The next morning, neither of them mentioned the night spent in each other's arms. Belle had woken up caged in his arms, her back against his chest, and a certain part of his anatomy pressing against her butt. Just thinking about it made her blush, which made her anger stir. In fact, everything about Beast made her want to hit him that morning. The way his messy hair hung around his face. The way he had offered his water to her. Even the way he had helped her up on his stupidly big horse. She padded Agathon's neck in silent apology for calling him stupid, even if it was in her head. But really, what business did Beast have, being so nice to her?

They had skipped breakfast because Beast had been eager to put more distance between them and the town, and Belle hadn't argued.

Beast had tried asking her questions. Questions about the fire, about what happened in the town, about the nightmare. But Belle had kept her mouth shut, and in the end, Beast seemed as angry as Belle.

They finally took a break at a small stream. Belle washed her face and arms, longing for a real bath. She also, with a bit of amusement, missed wearing the pants. Riding in a long skirt was not easy, and she constantly ended up with her legs exposed or the skirt tangled uncomfortably.

"Let's walk for a bit," Beast said, and Belle a bit reluctantly agreed. Her feet were sore from running, but she didn't want to mention it. He would probably just use it as an excuse to lecture her about how wrong it was that she ran. And honestly, she could use some distance from him. Sitting so close, having his body touching hers all the time, proved to be just another thing that made her angry. She sighed and picked up a wildflower. It was a soft pink, and she carefully twirled it between her fingers.

"What happened to your mother?" Beast suddenly asked.

Belle looked at him with narrowed eyes. Why did he want to know about her mother? But honestly, the quiet was getting to her. Neither of them had said a word for hours. "She died when I was ten."

"I'm sorry," he said. "Was it the fever?"

It was a reasonable assumption. So many were taken by fever every year. "No, she died when the monster came."

Beast's face flashed with anger before falling back into a neutral mask. "And your sister?"

"She's married. Moved away from the village the first chance she got." Away from Belle, but she didn't say it out loud. It would just lead to questions she didn't want to answer.

"You loved her a lot." It wasn't a question but a statement.

"Yes, but how did you know?" She had loved her

sister. More than life itself.

"I remember the way you pushed her behind you when I found you in the cave up in the mountains. You were such a small thing." He looked at her with a grin, and Belle rolled her eyes. Yes, yes, she was still small. She hadn't grown much in height since that day. She had been the tallest girl among her friends. Then the attack came, and everyone started to grow taller than her.

"And yet, you faced me with fierceness. I'm sure even at ten, you'd have swung a mean fist. Where did you learn to fight?"

"I read about it in books." She hesitated, a blush burning her cheeks. "I also snuck in and watched when there was a boxing match in town."

"Boxing?" Beast raised an eyebrow, but she saw the smile hiding in his eyes.

"Mhmm. Men would come from all the neighboring villages and gather in this little closed courtyard behind the tavern. Then some of them would take off their shirts, and they would box. Some of them were really bad, but sometimes it would get really bloody." Belle realized that maybe she shouldn't sound quite as excited about blood and fighting, but Beast didn't seem like he cared.

Beast threw his head back and laughed. Belle just kept surprising him. She had spent the whole morning glaring at him and looking like she wanted to stab him in the back. He had been surprised when she actually answered his questions since she had been so tight-lipped all day. But hearing her talk about boxing with such enthusiasm. It transformed her into a whole other person.

"You're a bloodthirsty little thing," he said.

"I am not," she said with a cute growl.

"Are you not? You've swung at me multiple times by now."

"You deserved it," she said with conviction.

"Watching boxing. And in the alley with those men." Beast could have cursed himself as soon as the words were out of his mouth. He could see how she shut down, and he wanted to grab and shake her. He finally had her talking, opening up to him, and now she had clamped shut again. With a sigh, he got them back on Agathon. They really couldn't get to the castle fast enough because this silence was getting tiring.

When they made camp for the night, Beast left Belle to make the fire while he tried to hunt something for dinner. He moved quietly through the forest, letting his senses take in everything. Scents wafted around him, and he followed the trails until he spotted a fat rabbit. He notched an arrow and let it fly. The rabbit collapsed to the ground, its legs twitching a few times before it stilled. Beast skinned and cleaned it with practiced moves while his mind roamed. When he returned to camp, Belle had a fire going, and Agathon was brushed to perfection. Belle sat by the fire, and he couldn't avoid noticing that she had placed their blankets side by side. He didn't mention it, just got the rabbit ready to roast.

They ate in silence, and Beast regretted his earlier words. He enjoyed the sound of her voice and the way she blushed when she said something she thought wasn't proper. He even enjoyed the way anger made her eyes flash. When it was time to sleep, Belle seemed to have regretted her decision to sleep beside him. Beast wasn't sure them sleeping this close was a good idea either. He needed to keep his distance from her. Needed to remember why he was taking her to the castle, and having her sleeping in his arms wasn't helping. He was already drawn too close to her. But he couldn't say no either if it meant helping her sleep. So he waited patiently, crouching by the fire, pretending to get it ready for them to sleep. He could see the struggle on her face, the war going on inside her. Then, with a deep sigh, she kicked off her boots and crawled under the blankets. Beast got up from the fire, kicked off his own boots, and crawled in beside her. She lay with her back to him, and he lay on his back, looking at the sky above them. The moon was gaining in size, and the stars stood above them. Soon the moon's call would reveal the truth, whether Belle wanted it or not. Beast's stomach clenched at the thought. He didn't want to know. He didn't want to be the one to take her life.

Belle rolled over, already asleep, and snuggled against his side. He wrapped an arm around her and kissed the top of her head.

"I don't know if you're my punishment or my salvation, Belle, but I don't want to let you go," he whispered into her hair.

Beast was woken by a kick to his knee. He growled at the pain and tried to grab Belle's flailing hands. She was mumbling and trashing, caught in another nightmare. He wrapped his arms and legs around her and held her as tight as he could.

"Shhh, Belle, it's okay. It's just a nightmare. Just listen to my voice. I'm not gonna let anything happen to you."

Belle finally relaxed and stopped fighting him. He let her go and just held her against his chest. He knew about nightmares. Two hundred years was a long time to collect things for his mind to twist into fears and terrors.

Chapter 7

The landscape was changing each day. The forest grew darker and wilder. The lush green was replaced with brown dirt and gray rocks. A few times, she had seen wolves between the trees, and not the smaller brown ones they had near her village. These were big gray beasts that blended into the surroundings. They never got close, but for once, Belle was glad she was sitting on Agathon, with Beast's reassuring presence behind her.

Beast led them from the small forest path they had been following and onto a road. It had once been a well-maintained road, paved with stones, but years of rain, weeds, and misuse had left it an uneven mess. Agathon perked up, his ears pointing forward and his gait picking up a bit of speed.

"Are we close to your home?" Belle asked, figuring the horse was happy to be on known territory.

"You'll see it once we get around the bend in the road," Beast said.

They had been slowly climbing up for the last two days, but Belle hadn't quite realized how high they were. When Agathon took them around the bend in the road, her breath caught in her chest, and she grabbed the rains and pulled, willing the horse to stop.

"What?" Beast asked.

"It's beautiful." The road had turned onto a cliff side, and the sudden drop offered them a look over the hidden valley below. The valley was guarded on all sides by mountain peaks rising far above them, standing like silent guards. The forest ran like tongues down the mountains and into the valley, but most of it was covered in grass. Horses, looking no bigger than toys, were grazing, and Agathon stretched his neck out and called for them. The horses raised their heads and called back.

"Where do you live?" she asked. She hadn't given it much thought, but she realized that maybe she should have. For all she knew, he lived in a tiny little hut.

"There." Beast caught her chin and turned her face, and she gasped at the sight that met her. A castle rose at the furthest part of the valley. Built from the same dark gray as the mountain stone, it looked like it had risen fully formed from the ground. Towers and spires twisted towards the sky, and she saw the setting sun glinting in big glass windows.

"You live in that?" Belle finally managed to ask.

"I am a prince, after all."

"A prince that's been lost for hundreds of years."

"So has this castle," he said and nudged Agathon to start moving.

Belle's mind was swirling. This was the first time he admitted he might be more than just human. Had he really been alive for hundreds of years?

The road twisted its way along the mountainside and into the valley, and they came out of the forest near the castle. Belle twisted around, trying to take it all in. Scary stone figures watched them from every corner and beneath the roofs. Big twisted rose bushes stood against the castle walls, covered in big red blooms. It wasn't the beautiful white castles from her fairytales, but she guessed a castle like this fit a man that might be a monster.

Beast stopped Agathon at the stairs leading to the big doors and jumped to the ground. Belle accepted his help to get down and was loath to let go of his hand, once standing on her own two feet. It was one thing knowing he was somehow an immortal being who had once been a prince. Not that he had said it outright, but he hadn't denied or hidden it either. But it had just been a loose concept. Something that was, but wasn't. Standing here in front of the castle suddenly brought it all home, making her feel very small and insignificant.

One of the big doors opened, and an older man walked outside. He was tall and thin, with white hair and a small white mustache. He wore dark pants, a white shirt, and a dark vest. He looked very much put together and in control. Belle glanced down at herself. The dress was crumbled, dirty, and had more than a few tears and spots. Her hair was a mess, and she desperately needed a bath.

"Lord Prince, it's good to see you home." The man gave a small bow to Beast before he turned inquisitive eyes toward Belle.

"It's good to be home, Potter." Beast indicated Belle. "This is Belle. She will be staying as my guest for the foreseeable future."

Belle nearly snorted at Beast referring to her as a guest, but she settled with rolling her eyes.

"Of course, sir."

A younger version of Mr. Potter came out from a side door. "Welcome home, sir," he said, but his eyes were on Agathon, assessing. Beast handed over the reins to his stallion over to the young man, and then they followed Mr. Potter inside. Belle tried to act as if walking into castles was something she did every day, but she only made it about three steps before she nearly stumbled over her own feet, trying to look at the ceiling. It was painted as an exact replica of the valley and the castle. Belle had never seen anything like it and wondered how the painter had managed to paint anything so far off the ground.

Beast grabbed her arm after that, and she dropped every pretense about not looking. As they walked through the castle, her eyes kept getting pulled from one item to another. The walls had glittering lamps spaced out, and she imagined how they would light the halls at night. A full set of armor stood in some of the alcoves, while others had twisted statues of men and creatures. Portraits hung between the lamps and the alcoves, showing the stern faces of men and women. The floors were polished wood, and when she glanced at the ceiling, she nearly stumbled again. The ceilings were painted in dark colors, with white stars making intricate patterns.

Beast finally stopped in front of a door, and Mr. Potter pushed it open.

"Your room," Beast said and gave her a gentle push

to make her step inside. Belle faintly heard the door close behind her, but her mind was busy trying to take it all in. A giant bed dominated the room. Covered in blue fabric and with more fabric strung between the four posts of the bed, it looked like the softest thing she had ever laid her eyes on. She ran her fingers over the fabric, then grabbed it and pulled it to her face feeling it against her cheek.

She walked around the room, running her hands over everything. A small desk stood near the windows, and a couple of glass doors led out to a small balcony overlooking the valley.

A dresser and a wardrobe were present too, both empty. A vanity with a silver mirror stood empty, with an intricately carved bench in front of it. A big fireplace was built into one wall, and a couple of big armchairs stood in front of it. The room felt bigger than her father's house.

Beast strode through the castle, heading for his own rooms, Potter following, ready to receive his orders.

"I take it the hunt was a success?"

"It was," he said.

"Good. And the woman?"

"An unknown, and I don't like the unknown."

"Should I put a guard on her?"

"No, she has nowhere to go." Beast hesitated. "Make sure she gets a bath. And send Camilla to the eastern tower. She should be able to find some dresses among my mother's old things. At least some of them should be fitting Belle. Though Camilla might have to shorten them a bit." A smile tugged at his lips. "And tell Mrs. Potter to prepare a formal dinner."

"Of course, sir. And should I send up a bath for you too?"

"Yes, thank you." Beast stepped into his room, closed the door behind him, and exhaled all the tension sitting in his body. He pulled off his dirty riding clothes and walked to the bed. He wanted to just collapse into it and sleep until morning. Belle's nightmares woke him several times each night, and he was feeling the lack of sleep. On top of that, they had traveled much slower than he would have preferred, and it had taken them longer to get home. There were only six days till the full moon.

A knock sounded on his door, and two stable boys walked in, hauling warm water for the bath. They were the youngest generation at the castle, but Beast knew every member of his staff. They were all born and raised within these walls. The only newcomers were the spouses married into the family, and even then, those men and women were often already part of Beast's extensive network of informants.

When the tub was filled, he sank into the scalding water and closed his eyes. He sat for a few minutes before he dipped below the water and washed the dust and grime from his face and hair. Once every part of him had been scrubbed clean, he leaned back again to enjoy the last few minutes of warm water. He heard Potter walk around in the room, but he didn't stir until the man cleared his throat.

"Your clothes are ready for you, sir. Do you wish a shave?"

"I'd appreciate it, Potter."

He stepped out of the bath and quickly dried. He wrapped the cloth around his hips and sat down to let Potter work. The man's skillful fingers quickly worked, and the scrape of the razor and the snip of the scissors were comfortingly familiar.

Once his beard had been trimmed back to a suitable length, and Potter had spent quite some time untangling his hair, Beast was left alone to dress. He looked at the clothes Potter had placed on his bed and sighed. Beast very much preferred his riding clothes, but Potter was forever trying to force him into more formal wear. He ran his fingers over the silver thread embroidery on the jacket, and with an annoyed growl, he grabbed the pants and pulled them on.

There was a knock on the door, and Belle opened it to find a young woman waiting outside, her arms full of garments and carrying a basket.

"Hello," Belle said and stepped back.

"Hello, miss, I'm Annelie." The girl smiled big and walked to the bed, depositing all the garments on it before placing the basket on the floor.

"What's this?" Belle asked and looked at the pile.

"The master thought you might need some fresh

clothes. They aren't quite in style, but they should do the trick." Annelie looked her up and down. "I was told we might have to do some alterations." She pulled out a sewing kit from her dress.

Belle pulled up the first dress. It was made from fabric so light that Belle had never felt anything like it. It was a deep green and had glittery beads all over the top. Belle didn't care if it was fashionable or not. It was the most beautiful dress she had ever seen.

The next was blue and more simple in both fabric and design, but still prettier than anything Belle had ever owned.

She looked through the rest of the dresses, and every single one was exquisite, but when she got to the last in the pile, her breath caught in her throat. The fabric was shimmering gold, and the skirt had so many layers it was like a waterfall of fabric. Belle desperately wanted to wear it. With a sigh, she put it back on the bed. There would never be a reason for her to wear a dress like that.

Instead, she picked up the blue dress. "Let's go with this one," she said and wondered where Beast might have gotten these dresses? Was there another woman living in the castle other than the servants? She wanted to ask, but it felt strangely intrusive and not really her place. Belle frowned at that. She was a prisoner. Granted, it was a very luxurious prison, but she had no doubt that if she tried to leave, she would be stopped. So why should she care about what was right?

"Is there a lady at the castle?" Belle asked.

"Oh, no, miss. Only the lord prince."

"So, where do all these dresses come from?"

"They were his mothers."

Belle swallowed and ran her hands over the dress again. His mother had to have died some hundred and fifty years ago, if not more. He had kept them safe all those years, and now he was letting her have them. Letting her alter them.

She didn't understand this kindness.

"Come, miss, let me help you put it on." Annelie took the blue dress from Belle's hands and put it on the bed. Belle had already showered, and her hair was a tangled mess of wet curls. Annelie quickly pinned it up and helped Belle into the dress. The fine fabric slid over her skin, and she nearly sighed from the pleasure. The dress wasn't too bad. A bit big all over, and of course, too long. Annelie quickly put in a few pins along the side seams before pulling over a footstool.

Belle dutifully got on it, and Annelie turned out to be a quite an effective seamstress. It didn't take her long before she had the dress hemmed and altered enough to fit Belle somewhat.

"I'll just take your measurement, miss, and then I'll alter the other dresses to fit."

"Thank you, but you don't need to trouble yourself. One or two dresses will be fine." Belle gestured to the two other, more simple dresses she had picked out.

"Oh, no, miss, the master was quite adamant that you have a full wardrobe."

Belle bit her lip not to snap at the woman. It wasn't her fault Belle's temper was running away with her, but really? Beast wanted her to have a full wardrobe of pretty dresses? Why? When would she ever need six ball gowns?

Annelie picked up the other dresses and hurried out the door, leaving Belle all alone again. She sighed, turned back to the bed, and noticed the basket. She had forgotten all about it, and apparently, so had Annelie.

She picked it up and dumped the content on the bed. A pair of black slippers, a brush, hairpins, Soft fabric to tie her hair, a comb, a small white box, and a hand mirror. She picked up the slippers first and slid them on her feet. They were a bit big, but nothing Belle couldn't handle.

Next, she picked up the brush, the comb, and the mirror. All three were silver, with little white pearls, and Belle couldn't stop running her hands over them. She carefully placed them on the vanity along with the hair ties and the hairpins.

She sat on the bed and picked up the small box. It was a simple box carved from wood. No ornaments, no carvings of any form. She carefully pried the lid free. Black fabric covered the insides, and on it lay a necklace. The chain was made from golden leaves, connecting and twining together. Roses unfolded between the leaves, big and full like the roses she had seen growing against the castle walls. And in the center of each rose was a glittering red stone.

Belle looked at it for a second before she slammed the lid closed. Anger surged through her. Did he think he could buy her compliance? Gift her with enough pretty things so she wouldn't mind being his captive?

For the first time since he saved her in the town, she thought about running away. Sneak out of the castle and just get lost in the woods.

She thought about the wolves in the forest and shook her head. *That's great, Belle. Let's run away, and if the wolves don't kill you, you're sure to hang in the nearest town.*

She threw the box on the bed and picked up the brush. With angry pulls, she started to untangle her hair. She just had to stay in these rooms. Avoid Beast as much as she could. Being around the man seemed to muddle her logical sense.

There was a hard knock on the door, and Belle nearly jumped out of her own skin.

"Belle?" Beast asked from the other side.

Belle stared at the door. Maybe if she just ignored him, he would stay away? No, more likely he would barge inside. "Yes?" she answered.

"Dinner will be served in an hour. I'd like for you to join me."

Dinner with Beast? A real dinner with real food and clean clothes? "I'm not hungry, but thank you."

"Belle, you need to eat something."

"Is that an order?" She was answered by low cursing and then the sound of Beast's retreating feet.

Chapter 8

Beast stood outside Belle's door, cursing the woman to hell. He had eaten dinner alone, and despite Mrs. Potter having outdone herself, he had been too angry to enjoy it. He had done everything he could for that woman. Saved her life multiple times, despite her insisting on putting herself in danger again and again. Brought her to his home and provided her with everything she needed. Instead of being grateful, she was sulking in her room.

Beast leaned against the door and heard her muffled cries. She was having another nightmare, and every fiber in his body screamed for him to go in there and help her.

He grabbed the door handle, but the door didn't budge. He stared at the door, his mouth opened in shock. She had actually locked him out? Damn that woman. Damn her all to hell. He was tempted to just throw her out of his home.

Beast breathed deeply and took a step back from the door. And then he smelled it. The scent of a predator. It was weak, almost not there, but still unmistakable. He stumbled back and sat down hard on the stairs. She was changing. It was no longer a question of if. When the full moon came, she would become one of the monsters.

He buried his head in his hands. By all rights, he should just kill her now. Kill her before she became a threat to anyone. But even as he thought it, he shook his head. He should, but he knew he couldn't. There was no logic behind it. Half the time, she ignored him, and the other half, she seemed ready to strangle him. Still, the thought of her getting hurt made his heart beat faster.

No, he wouldn't kill her. He would wait until the full moon. Until she was gone, and only the monster remained. And in the meantime, he would make sure the last few days she had left were as happy as they could be. Even if it meant sitting outside her door, hoping to convince her to come outside. With a sigh, he pushed to his feet and went to bed.

Belle bolted upright in bed, grabbing the bedding so hard her fingers hurt. Her ears rang with the screams from her nightmare, and when she wiped her face, her fingers came away smeared with tears.

I'm clearly losing my mind. It has to be the only explanation for these nightmares.

She forced herself to take deep breaths. The other nightmares had been scary but understandable. Related to things that had actually happened, though twisted and strange.

71

This nightmare, though, was nothing like that. She stepped from the bed and to the window, looking out over the valley. A half-moon hung in the dark sky, casting a ghostly glow over everything.

She didn't understand this nightmare. She had often had nightmares about the monster that took her, but this time she was the monster. She was the one tearing flesh from bones. She was the one enjoying the feel of hot blood down her throat.

She hugged herself and turned away from the valley. It was just a bad dream. Probably brought on by the last week's stress and turmoil. She tried to dispel the images from her mind, but she could almost feel the hot blood filling her mouth. Her stomach growled with hunger.

Belle looked towards the door. Everyone had to be asleep by now, so maybe she could sneak out, find the kitchen and get some food. She hadn't eaten since that morning, and it was probably hunger that twisted her nightmares. She pulled the blue dress over her head and bound her hair back before leaving her room on bare feet.

She had no idea where the kitchen might be and walked the halls aimlessly. Every corner she turned and every room she stepped into revealed new art and curious objects, and Belle got distracted from her goal. Most of the paintings were of landscapes, but some were of people too. She stopped in front of a full-figure painting of a woman wearing the dress Belle was currently wearing. The woman had long black hair, thick and glossy. Her lips were painted red, and her startling eyes were two different colors. One blue, one golden. This had to be Beast's mother.

She looked kind and young.

"Hello, young miss."

Belle turned with a start, looking at the newcomer. A plump, old woman with gray hair and kind eyes looked back at her. She wore a white nightdress, a brown shawl, and a pair of fussy slippers.

"Oh, hi," Belle said.

"Are you lost?"

"Ummm, I was just looking for the kitchen."

"Well, you can follow me then. I was heading there myself."

The old woman led Belle through the castle and down a set of stairs into a big kitchen. It smelled of bread and herbs, and Belle's stomach growled loudly.

"Oh dear, let's get you some food."

"Oh, you don't have to trouble yourself."

"Nonsense, it's my job to keep everyone fed."

"Your job?"

"Yes, dear, I'm the cook, Mrs. Potter."

Mrs. Potter directed Belle to a table, and before Belle could protest, a platter with cheese, meat, bread, and fruit was placed in front of her, along with a big mug of a steaming drink.

"What's this?" Belle asked. She sniffed the mug and studied the brown liquid. It smelled sweet.

"Hot chocolate, dear," Mrs. Potter said.

Belle gaped at the mug. She had read about hot chocolate but never thought she would get a chance to taste it. It was ridiculously expensive and hard to get your hands on.

"No, I... I can't accept this."

"Why not, dear?" Mrs. Potter asked, sounding genuinely puzzled.

"Because this is way too much. The price of this..." Belle trailed off when Mrs. Potter started to laugh.

"Oh, sweet child, you don't have to think about that. I drink a cup every night. The lord prince brings it home from his travels."

Belle couldn't wrap her head around the extravagance of it all. A servant drinking hot chocolate every night? Carefully she lifted the mug to her lips, blew on the hot liquid, and took a small sip. Sweetness exploded over her tongue, along with a slightly bitter taste. She held back a moan and took another sip.

"So, dear, what do you like to do?" Mrs. Potter asked when Belle finally put the empty mug on the table next to her empty plate. She was full, content, and felt sleep tugging at her.

"Like to do?"

"Yes, of course. You can't just sit in your room all day, hiding."

Belle looked down at the table. That was exactly what she had been planning to do.

"I understand this must be a weird situation for you, but I promise the master is a good man. He would not want you to hide away."

"Who cares what he wants," Belle said in annoyance, her need to voice her thoughts finally breaking free. Mrs. Potter was a nice woman. Maybe she would understand. "No matter how many pretty things he offers me, I'm still a prisoner at this castle."

"A prisoner, dear? What gave you that idea?"

Belle pushed from the table, staring at the old woman. "So, you're saying I can just leave right now, and Beast wouldn't drag me back?"

"I think the master would be worried if you left. As I understand it, you're hunted for witchcraft. Being accused of being a witch is very bad in this region."

Belle stalked back and forth behind the table. "That's what he said too. That he did it to keep me safe. But I don't believe that. No one is this nice to a stranger for no reason."

"Maybe he has his reasons," Mrs. Potter said. "Maybe he's been alone for a long time, hiding, and saw something of himself in you. Or maybe it's something else that he isn't ready to share yet. Whatever his reasons, don't punish yourself over them."

Belle sat down again, looking at Mrs. Potter. She was right. Belle was only punishing herself. She was in a fantastical castle, surrounded by beautiful things, and she had decided to hide in her room.

"I like books," she finally said. "And baking." Baking was one of the few chores she had enjoyed.

"Well, you are welcome to come down here and bake as much as you enjoy." Mrs. Potter took the plate and mugs and put them in the sink. "But, now it's time for bed."

"I don't know what to do," Beast almost yelled as

he stalked back and forth in the kitchen. He had tried talking to Belle that morning and been ignored again. He had tried inviting her on a walk outside and been ignored. When she ignored his offer to join him for lunch, he had stalked into the kitchens, hoping Mrs. Potter could give him some advice.

"She's scared and confused," Mrs. Potter said.

"And she won't let me help her. She had a nightmare, and all I could do was listen to her cry and whimper."

Mrs. Potter closed the cupboard hard, making the china inside rattle. "You listen to me, boy."

If Beast hadn't been so angry, he would have smiled at the 'boy.' For all she looked to be the oldest, Beast was a couple of hundred years her senior.

"She is a prisoner in this castle."

Beast opened his mouth to protest, but the old woman just kept on going.

"I know you haven't locked her up, but where would she go? She has no money, no clothes to call her own, and every city and town will have her name and picture hung on the church door. And you be honest with me now, would you really let her go if she wanted to leave this place."

Beast glared at her before looking away towards the fireplace. He couldn't look the old woman in the eyes because she would see the truth. Even if Belle begged him, he couldn't let her go. She was his prisoner until the day he would have to kill her.

"She likes reading," Mrs. Potter said with a smile. "Maybe bring her a few of your books. If nothing else, it will keep her occupied while she hides out in her

76

room."

"She comes from a small village, Mrs. Potter. She might not be able to read." As soon as the words left his mouth, he remembered her telling him she had read about fighting.

"Oh, she can read. She told me so."

"When?"

"Oh, late last night. Well, technically early this morning. I found her walking around in the halls on my way to make myself a cup of tea. She was starving the poor thing."

"If she had joined me for dinner, she wouldn't have been starving."

"Don't be mean. Now, go on with you and let this old woman work in peace."

Beast leaned down and kissed her fluffy white hair. He hated to see the passing of time. He remembered when Mrs. Potter had just been little Valerie. Running around and picking flowers in the garden. Now her life would soon be over, and her daughter would take her place as the head of the kitchens.

Belle had decided she wanted to enjoy her time at the castle. Her talk with old Mrs. Potter had helped put it in perspective. Prisoner or not, she would be a fool to not take advantage of the opportunity offered. But there was no way she would do it with Beast. She had ignored all his invitations, and she wasn't blind to the way he had almost growled in annoyance when she refused his last offer to join him for lunch.

She sat on the wide windowsill, wearing the green dress. Annelie had been by with a few more dresses, and Belle had asked her to help with her hair. It was now pinned on top of her head in braids and curls.

There was a knock on the door, and she expected it was Beast coming to try and invite her out for another activity. She waited, but there was no one talking to her, no noise outside the door.

"Come in," she called when the silence dragged on. The door didn't open, and Belle was finally drawn towards it. She pressed her ear against it but didn't hear anything, so with a mental shrug, she pulled it open.

A serving cart stood right outside the door. A plate of small cakes waited along with a pot and a cup made from fine porcelain painted with flowers. And beside it all, lay a book. Mrs. Potter must have remembered she liked to read.

Belle grabbed the cart's handle, pulled it into her room, and closed the door. The warm scent of cocoa and the sweet scent of the cakes rose from the tray, but she ignored both and picked up the book.

It was bound in heavy leather and had gold letters on the front. She couldn't help the smile when she read the name *La Belle et la Bête.* She hugged it to her chest for a second. She hadn't allowed herself to think about that day, but holding the book brought the memories forth. She wiped the tears from her face. Mr. Tobias had been the only person to never turn his back on her, and to have him stand there while she was bound naked to a pole made her stomach sour.

She looked at the book again and laughed through the tears. She had been thinking that even being kidnapped and locked in a castle would be better than her life, and here she was. Locked in a castle and held prisoner.

She carefully placed the book on the windowsill, poured herself a cup of hot chocolate, and picked two of the small cakes. She curled up on the windowsill with her treats and started reading her book.

She was almost at the end of the book when a piece of paper fluttered to the floor. Belle thought it might be a loose page and jumped to grab it. But it wasn't a page from the book, but a note.

No one should suffer alone.
When darkness falls, my arms are open.
All you have to do is knock.

Belle crumbled the note in anger and threw it on the ground. It wasn't Mrs. Potter who had brought the book but Beast. And now he had the audacity to invite her to his bed. Sure, she had slept in his arms while they traveled, but that was different, right? They had both been fully dressed and alone in the woods. Sleeping with him in a bed in his castle was more than just crossing the bridge away from proper behavior. It would be to burn it down.

Chapter 9

Beast was on the edge of sleep, caught in the state where the mind floats free, when a soft knock jerked him back to reality. The door opened, and light spilled inside. He lay still on the bed, watching as Belle tiptoed inside. She wore a long cotton nightdress, covering her from neck to toe. In fact, the dress was so long that she had the front clutched in one hand, the other carrying a lighted candle. She blew out the candle just inside the door, placed it on the little table, and closed the door, plunging the room into darkness. It didn't take his eyes long to adjust to the darkness, the moon casting enough light to let him see as Belle walked to the edge of the bed. He didn't say anything, just threw the covers back and waited. He felt her gaze trail over his body. He only wore a pair of sleep pants, and he wondered if that might be a mistake because the way Belle was looking at him made his mind run in directions he rather wouldn't go.

With what sounded like the most annoyed sigh he had ever heard in his life, Belle crawled into bed. He pulled her close and wrapped them both in the blankets.

Belle gave a content sigh and dropped off to sleep.

Beast lay awake, breathing in the scent of her hair, trying hard to ignore the feel of her body pressed against his. He had no idea how he was gonna let her go when the full moon took her. He held her tighter and pressed his lips to her hair. He would do what he had to, but it would shatter him to do so.

Belle couldn't stop running her hands over the dress. The red fabric teased her fingers, so soft and cool to the touch, and she had never felt anything like it. She picked up the red rose that had arrived with her breakfast tray. There had also been a note from Beast, saying he had to leave, but that he hoped she would enjoy the day.

Belle was looking forward to a day of exploring the castle. With Beast gone, she felt free to go where ever she wanted.

She had woken up in his arms, her head pressed against his naked chest. She had run her hand up his side before realizing what she was doing and had nearly fallen to the floor in her haste to move away from him. Beast's rough laughter had followed her as she fled the room. She couldn't allow herself to go to him again, or she would end up like the silly girl in her book. Beast was simply too kind, and if she wasn't careful, she would start liking him. *Falling for your captor? You're gonna end up as dimwitted as those girls in the books.*

Belle walked up the narrow staircase, one slow step after another. Each of the balusters was shaped like branches from a tree, but Belle had noticed that tiny carved animals were hiding among the branches, and she was trying to spot them all as she made her way up into the tower. Her attention, though, was divided between the banister and the wall. Big windows cut into the wall, showing her breathtaking views of the valley, the forest, and the setting sun. And between the windows hung paintings. But while the other paintings she had seen so far were portraits or landscapes, these were filled with fantastical scenes. Fairies in a meadow, colorful animals, floating mountains.

Belle wasn't sure what she had expected to find in the tower, but the room she stepped into wasn't it. There was no furniture, no carpets, and no paintings. Just a round room with a breathtaking view out of the big windows that filled half the wall. And there, in the middle, was a pedestal with a glass top. And in it floated a dead flower stem. Dark brown dried leaves covered the bottom. Belle stared at the dead rose but didn't walk closer. For some reason, it made her feel sick to her stomach to look at it. Instead, she walked the perimeter of the room and stopped at four long grooves in the wall. Something had cut into the stone, something strong and sharp. She looked around the room and found more of those groves. As if some angry animal had been raging. Belle hugged herself and backed away from the wall and the evidence it showed.

She had known he was one of the monsters. Had

known it since he saved her in the town, but her mind had been tricked by his kindness to forget it. But there was no forgetting it now. She bumped into the pedestal and turned around, a scream caught in her throat. Glass shattered against the floor, and the dead flower stem and leaves burst into dust as they came into contact with the air. She covered her mouth as a gust of wind carried them away.

Something was behind her, and she whirled around to see Beast standing in the doorway, looking at her with glowing eyes.

"What have you done?" he growled and stepped closer. He grabbed her arm, but Belle twisted loose, her dress ripping as she fled the room. She ran down the stairs, jumping the last steps and nearly tripping over the dress in her hurry to get away.

She didn't care about wolves or witches. All she knew was that she had to get away. Get away from this castle, away from Beast.

"Belle, wait," Beast called behind her, but she ignored him and tore out the big doors. The burning was back inside her as if a fire was licking against her flesh from the pit of her being. She screamed and tore at her dress, shredding the fabric under her hands.

She doubled over, pain ripping her apart.

Beast swore and followed Belle. He hadn't meant to get angry, to growl at her, or grab her. But that rose

83

was his last connection to the one who did this to him. His reminder to never give up on finding her.

He ran out of the castle, shouting to Potter to lock all doors. The full moon was still days away, but he wasn't taking any risks.

Beast ran through the forest but stopped when his nose caught a scent that couldn't be true. Monsters had a distinct stench about them. They smelled sick and twisted. But this scent. He hadn't smelled it in hundreds of years, and still, he remembered it clear as day. He had smelled it the first time he had shifted. The smell of strong magic.

He crept through the forest, keeping his senses open. If the witch was near, he would not let her get away. Something glowed up ahead between the trees. He moved closer and stopped when he saw the torn rags of one of his mother's gowns. He slowly moved to the edge of the clearing and knelt down to look out from under the low-hanging branches of the pine trees.

A beast was slowly coming to its feet, shaking out its fur. Big and dark, it looked around the forest with a single glowing red eye as if someone had placed a burning piece of coal into the beast's face. The other eye was white and unseeing, cut through by a scar. The scar started in the middle of the beast's forehead and ended somewhere below the muzzle.

It couldn't be. Those who turned were monsters. Raving mad and trapped between man and monstrosity. Only he, Beast himself, cursed by magic all those hundreds of years ago, turned into a beast like this. But there was no denying what he saw or the strong smell of magic that wafted off the beast.

Beast grabbed the knife at his belt, designed to be long enough to penetrate deep into a monster's chest. He hoped he didn't have to use it. If Belle had turned into a monster like him, no matter how improbable, he should be able to reason with her.

He stepped out from his hiding place, and the beast turned towards him.

"Easy, Belle. It's okay. I know you're confused, but everything will be okay." He kept his voice low and even, hoping to keep her from running. The worst she could hurt in this area was a few rabbits. But the horses weren't that far away, and in this shape, it would take her only a couple of hours to reach the nearest city.

Belle lowered her head to the ground, her ears pinned back flat, and growled, the sound vibrating in his chest, calling to his own beastly side. The long hair on her back stood up and started to glow, making it look like her back was on fire. "Easy, nothing's going to happen to you." He crouched down and met her glowing eye. "Belle, you're in control. Don't let the beast rule you. I know it's hard, but you can take charge."

Belle shook her head, took a step back, turned, and fled between the trees. Beast swore and ran after her. He had to stop her.

He ran after her, using every ounce of his strength to keep up. To his surprise, she didn't head for the horses, even though their scent was clear in the air, or run towards the town. She was running up, heading into the mountains.

Beast heard snarling and growling up ahead and

sped up. When he reached Belle, she was tearing into something small. Rabbit, his nose told him. Big claws dug into the ground, a bloody muzzle snapped, and another rabbit was devoured. She must have found a rabbit hole.

As she ate, the stench of magic dissipated, and Belle seemed to settle down a little. Beast took that as his cue to try again.

"Hey, Belle. Did the rabbits taste good?" He kept his distance, knowing just how fast a beast like her could move. She whipped around, but she didn't look quite as angry as before. One ear pointed at him, listening.

"That's it, girl. Let the anger go. Once you relax, I can help you shift back." He dared a step closer and finally allowed himself to really study her. She was big, almost as big as he was in his beast shape. But she was black and dark gray, where he was white and light gray. Her fur looked soft, and he wanted to reach out and run his fingers through it. He still had no idea how she existed, but seeing her caused a longing to stir in his chest. He had spent so much time alone, and even as he never wanted another person to carry his curse, he couldn't help feeling a strange kind of happiness from it.

Something stirred the bushes behind him, and he barely had time to throw himself to the side as Belle jumped forward to hunt the lone rabbit that had escaped the massacre.

He hadn't been quick enough, and pain flared up his arm where a few of her claws had caught him. He clamped his hand over it, but he could still feel the blood well to the surface and wet the fabric of his shirt.

Belle turned to him with a snarl, and he knew he was in deep shit. As much as the human part was in control, basic instincts were still much stronger when in the beast form, and Belle didn't seem to be much in control. Her instinct to go after bleeding prey would override everything. He didn't want to hurt Belle, but he might not have a choice right now.

Belle took a few steps closer and then collapsed to the forest floor. Finally. Beast took a deep breath and pushed to his feet. His first change had gone pretty much the same. Wild panic, anger, and confusion, and then he passed out and slept for hours. When he woke up again, he had been back to human, and it had all felt like a bad dream. Except he was naked in the forest.

He walked over to Belle and ran his hands through her fur. Here's hoping she turned back too, or he would have difficulty carrying her.

Chapter 10

Pain beat in her head, like a hammer striking her to the beat of her heart. She swallowed, her mouth dry like sandpaper, and carefully opened her eyes. She gave a relieved sigh when the room was dark, with only the weak light of a torch to cast a few rays of light through the room. She blinked against the darkness, trying to remember anything.

The smell of mold and musty straws filled her nose, and she definitely wasn't in a bed. Belle carefully sat up, moving slowly so her headache wouldn't get worse. It felt like any fast movement might make her sick.

She looked around and blinked, shocked when she saw the bars. Not on the windows, cause the room didn't have any, but the wall. One of the three walls was made of thick bars. Her heart skipped a beat. Did the witch hunters get her? Oh god, were they going to kill her? Torture her?

Why couldn't she remember?

And gods, she was so thirsty. She licked her dry lips and tasted the blood on them. Had she hurt herself? She looked down at herself - her very naked self - and fear coursed through her. Blood splattered her hands, arms, and chest.

"No. No." Her voice was high and shrill as she pushed into the corner, rubbing frantically to remove the dried blood. Memories came back, then. The pain, the fear, the anger. The need to hunt and taste fresh blood on her tongue.

Belle curled into a ball, hiding her head against her knees as loud sobs tore from her. She couldn't be one of the monsters. She couldn't. She just couldn't. Her whole life, she had been hated for her scars. People had feared her. But Belle had held her head high, knowing they were wrong. But they weren't wrong. They had all been so very right.

"Easy, girl, I got you."

Belle looked up, startled, thinking she was all alone. Beast? He was here?

"Come here."

Big hands grabbed hers, and she met Beast's blue eyes, filled with worry and understanding.

She crawled over to the bars, never letting go, and let him wrap her in his strong arms. Even with the bars between them, she had never felt this safe.

"I know it's scary, but I'm right here, and I promise nothing will happen to you. Just let it all out."

And she did. She buried her face against his warmth and cried. She cried for her childhood. For the dreams that had been stolen away that night so long ago. She cried for the girl she had been and the woman she was turning into. And mostly, she cried, because who could ever love a monster like her?

Strong fingers ran through her hair, gently massaging her aching head. Beast pushed a flask into her hands, and she greedily drank till it was empty, and then she cried some more. When she had run out of tears, and her spirit was just a hollow place where hope used to live, she looked up at him.

"Did I kill anyone?" She held her breath. If she had taken a life of some innocent man or woman, she would beg him to kill her.

"No, Belle, no. Just a few rabbits." He was sitting on the floor, pressed against the bars, one hand still running through her hair. "Here," he said and turned just enough to grab something beside him, his hand never leaving hers. "I brought you some of your clothes. I know it can get cold down here. I also brought some blankets for you."

"Can I- can I please come out?"

Beast's face went flat as if he had to force himself away from whatever emotion her plea lit within him. "I'm sorry, but it's too dangerous. You're too dangerous." He growled deep in his chest, and pushed from the floor, stalking back and forth in front of the cell.

"I don't know why this is happening. This, this shouldn't be happening." He stopped, grabbed the bars, and stared straight at Belle. She looked back at him, her heart beating too fast.

"When I changed the first time-" he hesitated and sat back down again. "It's close to the full moon, and you're likely to shift again without meaning to. It's safer for everyone if you stay here."

Belle clutched his arm again. Was she a beast like him now? She remembered the monster she had seen that night she was taken. It had been ugly and twisted.

Not a man but not an animal either. Trapped somewhere in between. Its body not quite fitting together as it should.

If she hadn't been looking at him at that exact moment, she would have missed it, but when she tightened her grip on his arm, a flash of pain crossed his face.

"Are you hurt?" she asked.

"No, it's nothing," he tried to avoid it, but she grabbed his arm and pulled up his sleeve. His arm was big and strong like his hands, with a light dusting of dark hairs on it and three deep furrows cut into the flesh where claws had ripped him open. Claws like those of a monster.

"I did this," she said and pushed away from him, horrified at what she had done.

"Belle, look at me."

His commanding tone broke through the rising panic, and she stared at him.

"You were hunting rabbits, and I got between you and your prey. Nothing would have happened if I had been smarter and kept my distance."

"Are you going to kill me?" she whispered into the darkness, not looking at him. She didn't want to see the answer on his face. He had killed the monster that had taken her. It was what he did. And now she had become one of them.

Silence spread between them, filling the darkness like a heavy blanket forcing the air from her lungs.

"I kill monsters, and you aren't one," Beast said.

Belle swallowed down a sob. She was. The blood on her hands and face was proof of it.

"But even if you were, I don't think I could."

"Why not," she said in a whisper.

"Belle, don't you know? I'm yours. I have been from the moment I saw you by that lake."

She shook her head as another sob tore from her. He couldn't. He couldn't love her because she was a monster. And she couldn't love him because he was a beast. She was the evil that walked the earth, and he was the evil that hunted it down. She buried her face in her knees and cried until sleep finally claimed her.

Beast hadn't meant to confess his feelings for her, but the words had seemed the right ones at the time. Seeing the way she had started to cry, he very much doubted he had been right. Beast walked back into the cells and found Belle writhing on the floor. He dropped the deer to the floor, fell to his knees, and reached for her, then pulled his hands back. The last thing she would want was his touch as the change took her. The change made the body feel like it was being flayed, and even the slightest touch made it feel like knives were being pushed all the way into the bones.

"Belle, listen to me. You have to let the magic flow. If you fight the change, it'll only hurt more. I know it's scary, but I know you can do it." He remembered his first shifts. How scary it had been when the magic took hold and reshaped his bones, grew fur, and claws.

He still didn't know how this could be happening.

Had she been cursed by the witch? A scream tore from Belle and her back lifted from the floor before she collapsed back on it, her body twisted in ways no human body naturally could. Beast started talking, hoping the sound of his voice might give her something to hold on to. He had never shifted with someone near him. Never had anyone to care for him, so he was in complete darkness as to what might help her.

"Belle, when I saw you in that forest. You were so beautiful. Strong, fierce, and ready to fight me if needed. I was so tempted to shift and run with you." Beast leaned against the stone wall and watched Belle. It wouldn't take long before she turned completely. She would be starving when that happened, which was why he had gone hunting. Fresh meat was the best.

"Did I ever tell you how I got cursed?" He hadn't. He was sure of it. "I was a stupid fifteen-year-old. In fact, it was my birthday. My mother had planned a big party for me, filled with people I didn't want to spend time with and expected me to mingle with them all, acting polite. I hated it because the grown-ups only acted nice to me because I was a prince. They didn't care about me. So, I sneaked out and hid in the gardens. And there I met an old woman. She was wrinkled, ugly, and smelled foul. I told her to go away, or I'd have the guards arrest her for trespassing."

Belle screamed, but the scream ended in a growl, and a beast rose to its paws.

"There you are."

Beast cut a big chunk of the deer and held it to the bars. Belle snapped it and swallowed it without even chewing it.

"Careful, or you'll just make yourself sick," Beast said and held out another piece. Belle carefully took it between her monstrous teeth and settled on the floor, ripping smaller chunks of it before chewing and swallowing.

"That's it. You're in control. Don't let the beast take over. Do you wanna hear the rest of my story?"

Belle looked at him briefly before going back to her meat.

"She told me I should learn to show some respect to my elders. And being in a foul mood already, I told her that a witch like her didn't deserve any respect. She laughed at that and rubbed her hand over her face, and suddenly she looked like a young woman. She told me that she would show me just how much of a witch she was. Then pain exploded in my body, and the next I knew, I woke up naked in the forest."

Beast kept feeding Belle meat through the bars, and while she kept eating like she had been starving for days, her ears flicked towards him, and sometimes she even paused and looked at him.

"Soldiers brought me back to the castle, and my parents hid me away here. The world couldn't know what I had become, or I would be burned on the stake. That first night here, the witch came to me in a dream and told me that I had five years to find my true love or I'd stay cursed forever. It's the families of the original soldiers still serving here at the castle. The few who are left. I guess in another fifty years, they will be gone too, and it'll just be me and this empty castle." And Belle now, too, but he didn't say it out loud. One step at a time.

He fed her the last piece of meat, but she paused with it between her fangs and looked at him before pushing it out through the bars toward him.

"Thank you, but these aren't really useful for raw meat." He tapped a finger against his teeth and pushed the meat back towards her. She picked it up again and stared at it, but once again didn't eat it.

"What's up? Are you full?"

She glanced at him, then back at the meat again. She sucked in air and, with a huff, sent a ball of fire over the meat. Beast nearly jumped to his feet. "What the?" he blinked and shook his head. It had taken him nearly a year to realize he had powers besides turning into a beast.

The meat was pushed through the bars again, and Beast picked it up, laughing. "Thanks. I guess I can try it now."

Chapter 11

Belle sat on a blanket, another blanket wrapped around her. She had stopped wearing clothes because when the shift took her, they hurt against her skin. She had even stopped being shy when Beast came to visit her cell, which he did often. In fact, she had stopped caring about most things. She felt numb, exhausted, confused, and angry all at once, which didn't make any sense, but that's how it was.

She hadn't talked much, but Beast never stopped talking to her. About his life, about being a beast, he even talked about the night she was taken. She had been lying on the stone floor, human again, floating in a haze of exhaustion but unable to sleep, when she felt his fingers trail over her calf. He had been tracing the scars left behind by fangs. She had always wondered why the monster that took her had saved her from rolling over the cliff side by biting her leg and dragging her back. But as she lay there, Beast's fingers lulling her into sleep, he told her he was the one who bit her. He was the one who had saved her life. Not just from the monster but from the cliff too.

Somehow, in the last three days, sitting behind these bars and listening to Beast talk and explain, she found she didn't hate him. At least, not as much as she had.

She had lost track of time. It all blurred together with the pain of shifting. She picked up the pitcher of water and sipped from it. Her own stench made her wrinkle her nose. That was another thing that had changed. Her senses seemed to have grown. She heard things she'd never heard before, like the footsteps coming down the stairs. The scent telling her it was Beast.

She wasn't sure she would ever leave these cells. Beast had told her he would let her out. That he wouldn't kill her. He had even talked about how much control she already had over her beast, though she didn't remember much when she took the other form. But could she trust that the man who had spent hundreds of years killing monsters would let one go free? But then, he insisted she wasn't a monster. Though what she was then, she didn't know.

"Ready to get out of here?" Beast asked as he stopped in front of her cell.

Belle looked up at him, not sure she had heard him right. "You're gonna let me out of here?" she asked.

Beast frowned back at her. "I told you I would."

She nodded, unwilling to argue the point and risk him changing his mind. Her legs wobbled under her as she tried to stand. It felt strange standing on two feet as if her body had forgotten how to do it.

"Easy. The weirdness will disappear once your body gets used to the shift."

Belle wiped her face, but she had no more tears to shed. She didn't want to get used to it, but she figured

97

she didn't have a choice. And she was tired of crying. Tired of the panic and fear.

Beast opened the cell door and hovered close to Belle, but he didn't offer her any help, and for that, she was grateful. She didn't need to feel any weaker than she already did.

Beast led her through the castle, which seemed empty of anyone else. Another thing Belle was grateful for. She didn't need Mrs. Potter, Annelie, or Mr. Potter to see her wearing nothing but a blanket and covered in days worth of sweat and filth.

He finally opened the door to her room, and if there had been any tears left in her, she would have wept at the steaming tub and the dress laid on her bed.

"I'll be right out here. Just call if you need me." And then Beast leaned down and placed a kiss on top of her head.

She cried then. A few fat tears running down her face.

The door closed behind her, and Belle made her way to the tub, letting the blanket fall to the floor. She grabbed a washcloth from the small table and, not caring one bit about the floor, wiped the worst grime from her skin before she made her way into the tub.

If there was a heaven, this had to be it.

Beast knocked on the door almost an hour after Belle had walked into her room. He had waited outside long enough to make sure she made it into the tub. Then he'd hurried to the kitchen and ordered a big tray of treats be made up and delivered to the library.

"Come in," a scratchy voice said from the other side. He opened the door and found Belle standing near the window wearing a pink dress, her wet hair curling around her head. He had never seen anyone more beautiful, and he wanted to tell her. But despite everything that had happened, he was smart enough to know Belle wouldn't appreciate it. Instead, he stayed by the door and said, "I have something I'd like to show you. It's your choice, of course."

Belle didn't look at him, just stared out the window. "Can we go outside?"

"If that's what you'd like. But I'd still like to show you something after."

They walked outside, and Belle seemed to shrug off some of the melancholy surrounding her when the first rays of the sun hit her face. He let her stand there on the steps, soaking it up, and watched her. She finally looked at him, and the beginning of a smile graced her lips.

"Can we say hello to Agathon?" She asked.

"Of course, but we might have to walk for a bit," Beast warned.

"I don't mind," Belle answered.

Beast took a chance and extended his arm. Belle stared at it for a moment, then placed her fingers on it. Beast fought his smile as he led her down the stairs and into the valley.

Belle stared at the horses grazing close to them. She had never seen so many big animals in one place. There were foals playing around in the tall grass. And horses of every color moved around, snorting and keeping an eye on everything.

Beast raised his head and whistled, and Belle watched as Agathon detached himself from the herd and ran over. Belle couldn't explain the happiness she felt by seeing the big stallion. And she very much ignored how her mouth watered when she smelled the warm scent of prey.

"It'll get easier," Beast whispered to her. He was standing right behind her, too close, and yet Belle wished he would put his arms around her and just hug her close. Hold her like he did in the night when she had a nightmare.

"When?" she whispered back. She didn't want to break the spell there seemed to lie over them.

"It's hard to say. I was so angry the first many years, so I never noticed. I ran away from here not long after I was cursed. Joined the wars."

"That must have been terrible."

"At first, I didn't care about anything. As often as I fought as a man, I would go out at night as the monster. Bring chaos and terror to the enemy camps."

"What about later," she asked. Agathon pushed his big head against her, and she stumbled. Beast's arms wrapped around her, steadying her. She leaned back against his chest and rubbed her fingers up and down Agathon's head.

"Later, I hated it. I hated the death and the sickness of it all. Men killing each other just so those in power could get more power."

"And yet, you kept killing."

"Not for long. I went back here after fifteen years of wars. Not that I could have stayed much longer. I had stopped aging a few years before. People would have started asking questions."

"But you still hunt the monsters."

Beast hugged her closer, and Belle swore he kissed her hair again, before stepping away from her. "The monsters are my fault and my responsibility."

"What do you mean?" she asked and turned to look at him.

"I didn't realize at first. But the men I fought and hunted as the beast during the wars. If they didn't die, they turned. It often took weeks or months. Long enough for them to be spread out, go home. I've been trying to clean up my mess ever since." The pain in Beast's voice pulled at Belle, and she put her hand on his cheek, making him look into her eyes.

"You were just a kid and didn't know what you were doing. Don't punish yourself for the evil doings of a witch." Belle was surprised that she heard the truth in her own words. He had been punishing himself for all these years.

"Can we go see what it was you wanted to show me?" she asked as Beast seemed too stunned to talk. Beast nodded, and together they walked back to the castle.

Beast opened the door to the library and had the pleasure of seeing Belle's face filled with shock and then awe.

"This is… how?… I…" Belle never finished her sentence, just walked into the library, her eyes darting around. Beast laughed and followed her inside. The small table in front of the big fireplace was set with tea, finger foods, and cakes. Beast walked over, poured himself a cup, and sat on the couch watching Belle explore. It took a couple of hours, and Annelie had come and gone unnoticed with a fresh pot of tea before Belle came over to the couch, her arms full of books.

"Are you going to read them all at once?" he asked.

"Well, no, but what if I never find them again."

"I don't think the library is big enough for books to disappear."

"Have you read them all?" she asked.

"Yes."

Belle carefully placed the books on the table and took the cup of tea Beast offered. She didn't stay sitting for long, though. This time, Beast followed as she explored another part of the library.

He enjoyed watching her. She would crouch down to look at the books on the lowest shelves, then stand on her toes to try and watch those highest up. A few times, she would ask him to pull down a specific book, but most of the time, she simply hiked up her dress and used the shelves as her own personal ladder. He fought to keep from laughing when it happened, but in the end, he laughed. Belle blushed, and an overwhelming need to grab and kiss her, to feel if the blush heated her skin, beat through him. He crossed his arms and leaned against the shelves to avoid grabbing her.

"What's this?" she asked as they stopped in front of the desk tucked into a corner. A big map hung on the wall, and the desk was overflowing with papers and notes.

"It's my work. Every sighting of a monster, every location of one I've killed." He couldn't keep every emotion out of his voice, though he tried. On that desk was a list of names. The names of every monster he had killed. Or the names they had carried when they had still been human.

Belle looked through a few of the notes, then turned to him. "If you really mean I'm like you and not them. I want to help you."

"Help me?" he asked in shock.

"Stop them. Hunt the monsters. To prevent any more innocent people from being killed."

Beast just nodded, unable to say the words he really wanted. He wanted to tell her he thought she was the bravest woman he had ever seen. That he would do everything he could to keep her safe. "Will you have dinner with me?" he asked instead.

Belle wore the golden dress. It was too much. Too pretty for a simple dinner. But when would she ever get a chance to wear anything like it again? Besides, she wanted to feel how it felt to wear something so beautiful at least once in her life. Annelie had helped her style her hair. It was curled on top of her head and fell in perfect ringlets around her face.

She opened the door when Beast knocked, and she took his arm. She had expected him to lead her to one of the many dining rooms in the castle, but instead, he led her outside.

"Where are we going?" she asked.

"It's a surprise."

They walked around the castle, following a path into the wilderness that belle was sure had once been a perfect garden and was now a mass of rosebushes, trees, and wildflowers. They rounded a corner, and Belle smiled at the sight. An old gazebo that looked to have been painted white at one point stood almost covered in rose bushes. The red roses filled the air with their perfume, and the tall trees standing guard above them cast everything in dancing shadows and light. It felt as if she had stepped into one of the fairytales from her books.

Inside the gazebo stood a table and two chairs. Candles burned in silver chandeliers hanging from the roof of the gazebo. Plates covered by silver domes littered the table, along with glasses filled with flowers and more candles. Two plates sat at one end, close enough together to feel intimate, not so close together it would feel forced.

Beast pulled out one of the chairs, and Belle sat down, careful not to get herself tangled in the big skirts. The dress wasn't designed for picnics, but she didn't care.

Beast sat in the other chair and grabbed a bottle from the table, and poured a golden liquid into her glass. Little bubbles rose inside the glass, and Belle could smell its sweet and bitter scent.

"Champagne," Beast said, holding out one of the glasses for her. She took it and let the liquid glide over her tongue.

"You look beautiful tonight," Beast said as he started to lift the silver domes, revealing the treats beneath.

"You're very handsome yourself," she said and felt her cheeks blush. It was true. He wore dark pants and a white shirt. He had let the top buttons remain unbuttoned, and for some reason, that just made him look even more handsome.

Dinner had gone better than Beast had ever thought possible. They had managed to spend hours together without any of them annoying the other, or so he hoped, at least. He couldn't stop staring at Belle. Sitting here in shadows and candlelight, the golden dress glittering when she moved, she took his breath away.

Her shift had brought a new glow to her, and while she still looked a bit tired and worn, he had no doubt she would find her way into this new world and carve out her own place, and if she let him, Beast wanted to be right there beside her.

"Dance with me," he asked and held out his hand. They had been talking about horses, how Belle wanted to learn to ride one herself, but the need to hold her close overrode everything else. She took his hand, and he pulled her close.

"There's no music," she said, but she didn't sound like she minded.

"I can get us some if you want it?"

Belle shook her head, and Beast smiled down at her. He placed one hand at her waist, and Belle seemed a bit unsure what to do with her other hand but ended up placing it on his upper arm. He started swaying around, humming a small tune he didn't even know he had remembered. He hadn't danced since before his curse, and Belle didn't seem like she had ever danced before either, so he kept it to the most simple moves, and yet it seemed magical.

Chapter 12

Belle woke when someone knocked on the door. She was wearing her long nightdress again and was tucked against Beast's naked chest. He had taken her to her room after they had danced and given her hand a chaste kiss before walking away. She had gone to bed but hadn't been able to sleep. What if the nightmares came back? What if the beast took over when she was sleeping? In the end, she had walked to Beast's room, and he had wrapped her in his arms and held her close until sleep finally found her.

"Shhhh, just go back to sleep," Beast said and got out of bed. Belle pushed up and tracked him through the dark room. He opened the door, and a light spilled over him. She heard whispering, but even her newly improved hearing couldn't make out the words. The door was closed again, and Beast got back to the bed.

"What was it?" she asked, unsure he would answer her.

"One of my people has heard rumors of another monster."

"Do you need to leave?"

"No, it's just a rumor. I need to hold it up against what other information I have. I would never be home if I had to chase every rumor that was spread about monsters." He wrapped himself around her again, and Belle fell back to sleep.

When she woke again, Beast wasn't in bed anymore. Heavy drapes covered the windows, and she had no idea what time it was. She stretched and climbed out of bed. Rubbing her nose, she pulled the curtains back and was met by the glaring high noon sun. Belle blinked against it. She had never slept this late before. With annoyance, she realized everyone would be up and about, and all she wore, was her nightdress.

She looked around the room and found a deep red dressing gown hanging on the back of the door. It wasn't perfect, especially because it trailed the floor behind her, but it was better than nothing. She made it back to her room, unseen, and hurried to get dressed.

She hoped Beast hadn't left to hunt whatever monster he had been notified about. She wanted to thank him for the night before. For the dinner, the dancing. She took a deep breath and let it out slowly. She wanted to thank him for everything. Despite the animosity she had shown him. Despite running away and refusing to answer any questions, locking herself in her room, and still needing him every night, he had stayed by her.

Belle found Beast in the library. She still couldn't believe so many books existed in one place. She wanted to stay here and never leave.

"Good morning, sleepy head," Beast said but didn't look up from the papers he was studying.

"You should have woken me up."

"I tried, and all I got was some growls before you pulled the blankets over your head."

Belle felt the blush heat her cheeks and was happy Beast wasn't looking at her.

"What are you doing?" Even with him facing away, she found she couldn't utter the words to thank him.

"Going through my notes, seeing if I can find anything cooperating the new rumors."

"Can I help?" Belle pulled a chair over and sat down at the end of the desk.

"Not with this, but if you really wanna help hunt them, you should read through these." Beast pointed to three stacks of notes and then at a bookshelf filled with notebooks and boxes.

"They are all about the monsters?" Belle asked. All that information. Beast had to have tracked hundreds of monsters over the years.

"Yes," was all Beast said.

Belle grabbed the first notebook on the shelf and started going through it. Beast got up from his desk and stretched, and Belle sneaked a few looks over the edge of the document she was reading. His hair was loose from his tie, and Belle had a sudden urge to grab it.

She looked up and met his gaze, and a smirk pulled at his lips. Fantastic, he had seen her staring. His face sobered, and emotions flittered in his eyes and over his face.

"You have to leave, but you don't want me to go with you," Belle said before he had a chance to speak.

"Yes. How did you know?"

"Because every thought flittered across your face."

"I know you want to go with me-"

"No. I mean, yeah, I do, but I'm not ready. Go, and I'll stay here and read through all this. There's enough to keep me occupied for at least a few days." Belle smiled up at him. She didn't want to be left behind, but she was smart enough to know she was far from ready to go anywhere. Her body still felt a little off, and the stray scent of horse that made its way into the castle made her mouth water. It wouldn't be safe for anyone. Still didn't mean she had to like it.

"I'll go pack, and then I'll be back to say goodbye."

Belle watched him go, and for some unexplainable reason, she wished he had kissed her before he left.

Beast was tired, dirty and his back hurt with every step Agathon took. He wanted to crawl into bed for a week and just sleep. Hug Belle close and let her scent chase the bad dreams away. It was a long time since he had seen such nightmares, at least outside of sleep. The monster had gone after a small settlement in the mountains. Just a few houses built close together. Everyone had been slaughtered. Husbands, wives, mothers, fathers, children. He was grateful that this had not been Belle's first encounter with the horrors of the monsters. If she didn't already hate him for creating the devil hounds he had spent hundreds of years chasing, she would after a sight like that.

His heart ached as he walked into the castle. He

didn't understand a word Potter said to him, and he left the old man standing at the steps, holding the rains of Agathon. He stopped outside Belle's bedroom, but despite the late hour, the room was empty. In fact, it smelled like it hadn't been used much during the days he had been gone. Had she been sleeping in his room? A pinch of guilt niggled in his chest. Her nightmares hadn't disappeared, and he had left her to deal with them alone. He walked to his bedroom, and Belle's scent lay heavy in the air. But the woman herself wasn't in the room. With a frown, he used his nose to hunt her down and found her in the library. She stood leaning over his desk, her hair a mess as if she had been running her hands through it. An empty mug and plate stood wobbling on the edge of the desk, and a few more tables had been moved over, all of them covered with notebooks and papers. The big map behind her on the wall, the one he had spent so many hours studying, was filled with needles.

"What you doing?" he asked when all he really wanted to do, was pull her into his arms. Belle turned and looked at him, but instead of answering, she frowned, worry clouding her eyes.

"What's wrong?" Belle walked over and stopped in front of him, looking into his eyes.

"Just let me hold you for a bit."

Belle nodded, and Beast pulled her close and just held her, feeling some of the tension drain from his body.

"You smell like blood," Belle whispered against his chest. "Is it yours?"

"Some of it," he whispered back.

111

Belle grabbed his hand and tugged him with her. She led them to the bedroom, and Beast followed, too tired to do anything but do as told. Belle pushed him down on the bed, and he sat heavily on it, letting her peel off his shirt. He had covered the wound with bandages as best he could, but the smell of fresh blood told him it had probably bled through.

Belle didn't ask what happened. She sensed that Beast didn't need her curiosity. She held back her gasp as she pulled the bandages away. Claws had ripped his flesh, leaving four deep furrows over his back. She had noticed the scars on his chest before but never the hundred scars crossing his back. She used his shirt and pressed it against the wounds, but Beast just grabbed her hand and pulled her into his lap.

"Don't. It'll stop bleeding soon enough. Just lie down with me."

Belle nodded, and Beast lifted her into his arms as if she weighed nothing and pulled the blankets down. He lay down, still holding Belle, and manhandled her until she was pressed against his chest. She bit her tongue not to complain. Whatever had happened, it had clearly been bad. She had never seen him this quiet.

They lay in bed for more than an hour before Beast started to speak.

"It killed everyone." He buried his face in her hair, and she hugged his head to her, afraid to hurt him if she held him like she wanted.

"There was a small settlement. You know, people hoping to build a better life somewhere new." There was a hitch in his voice, and Belle pushed herself higher in bed, so she could better hug him.

"It killed the kids, all of them. Ripped them from their beds and tore into them right there. There was a crib." His voice hitched, and Belle felt tears wet her neck.

"It's gonna be okay," Belle said and ran her fingers through his hair.

"It's my fault. I created the monsters, and now those babies and kids are dead because of me."

"No. Beast, listen to me." Belle grabbed his hair and pulled his head back until their eyes met. "You didn't create the monster you hunted these past few days."

"Of course I did. I already told you-"

"That you were cursed. I know. But I've been doing some research, and I discovered something." Belle grabbed his hand and pulled until he was on his feet. She had thought he needed her care, but perhaps he needed something else instead.

They walked back to the library, Belle still holding his hand. She walked straight up to the map and started to explain.

"I was reading your notes when I started noticing that something just didn't add up. So, I got some of Annelie's pins." She pointed at a grouping of pins. "Look. It's like rings in water, spreading out from this area. And look, here's another cluster with another center." She grabbed a paper she had worked on earlier and held it out to him. "And as far as I can figure out, with a bit of help from Mr. Potter and the books, every cluster corresponds with a lost prince."

Belle turned and looked up into his eyes. She needed him to understand this. It wasn't his fault. "I think the witch has been cursing princes all through the kingdoms, and each prince has started a chain reaction of monsters."

Beast walked over to the map and ran his fingers lightly over it, tracing the ring pattern with a finger. "I'm not on this map," he said.

"You fought enemy soldiers. If you turned someone into a monster, they would have left for their homes after."

"How do you know which monster belongs where?" he asked.

"I don't, not for sure. I started marking down where you had killed monsters. When I realized that they seemed to form into clusters, I tried to figure out why. It was actually Mr. Potter that pointed out about the lost princes."

Beast grabbed her into a giant hug, lifted her, and spun her around. "Thank you," he whispered in her hair.

"I told you that I would help."

"That you did."

Beast finally put her back on her feet, and she looked up at him with a smirk. "Now I just have to get ready to go on adventures with you. Then we can try and figure out where this witch is hiding."

Chapter 13

"I can't do it," Belle growled and shook out her hands. Why was this so hard? She should be able to do it, but no matter how hard she tried, and no matter how many times Beast tried to talk her through it, she couldn't force the shift.

"You're trying too hard," Beast said from the fallen log he was sitting on.

"Not concentrating enough, concentrating too much, trying too hard, not trying hard enough... can you make up your mind?" Belle kicked a branch and cursed loudly when it flipped and hit her shin.

"Belle, stop. Take a deep breath and come sit here with me."

"Why can't I do this?"

"Because there's a long time until the full moon."

"You can do it," she growled.

"And I've had hundreds of years to practice. You've had fourteen days."

"But we're leaving tomorrow." Belle's stomach clenched at the thought. She didn't feel ready to go anywhere. She could hardly ride, the horses still made her mouth water, and she couldn't fight or shift. She should stay home and let Beast leave, but the thought of him leaving without her made her stomach cramp even worse. If he was going after the witch, she was going with him.

"We can wait a bit longer," Beast said and pulled her into a hug. It was something he had been doing more and more. Touching her. Ever since he came back from his last hunt, something had shifted between them, and Belle wasn't so blind that she didn't realize it was her doing it. Somewhere along the way, she had stopped blaming Beast. Oh, she still had plenty of anger, but it was directed in the right direction. Mostly at the witch, who had hurt so many people with her curses.

"No, we can't wait any longer. You've gotten three notes about sightings in the last week. I won't let anyone get hurt because I was scared, and I'm not letting you go alone."

Beast kissed her hair and stepped back. "Okay, if you're sure."

"I am."

"We better get ready to leave then," Beast said.

"I need something else than dresses to wear."

"Like what?"

"Pants. I can't ride in these." Belle pulled at the skirt swirling around her legs.

"We have side saddles you can use."

"I'd prefer pants."

"I'll get you some, then, but we might have to bring a dress or two for you."

Belle grabbed a handful of curls. "We could just cut it off. Pretend I'm a boy."

Beast started to laugh, and Belle glared at him.

"Sweetheart, even with no hair, no one would ever believe you to be a boy." Beast sobered up and ran a hand down the side of her face. "Besides, we need the hair to help hide these."

Of course, the scars. How had she forgotten?

"Hey, I don't care about the scars." Beast grabbed her chin, and Belle was forced to meet his gaze. He leaned down and gently kissed the scar on her cheek. The air caught in her throat, and for a second, her mind went blank, but when Beast pulled away, Belle woke from her daze. She grabbed a lock of his hair and pulled him back down again. She had read about plenty of kisses in her books, but it was one thing reading about it and quite another doing it. Her kiss was clumsy, having no idea what she was supposed to do, but then Beast took over. With a growl, he pulled her closer, one arm around her waist, the other in her hair. He tilted her head a bit and licked her lips, and Belle eagerly opened for him. She still had a hand in his hair, and she grabbed a handful of his shirt with the other, needing to keep him close. Heat rushed through her, not the heat of the shift, but a fire just the same. It pooled in her stomach and made her fingers tingle. She wanted him closer, wanted to feel his hands on her burning skin. She was fire, and he was ice.

The taste of him swirled over her tongue. The tangy taste of apples, the sweetness of the cider he had been drinking, and underneath the taste of him.

Beast's hands slid down her back and grabbed her ass, and he lifted her up, pressing her back against a tree. He kissed across her jaw and down her neck, and Belle gasped for air. She wanted more. She wanted everything. She pulled at the buttons of his shirt, needing to get to his skin. Beast grabbed her hands and pinned them against the rough bark above her head.

"Belle, stop," he growled against her neck.

"No," she breathed and bit the skin on his neck, leaving a red mark. Beast had a leg wedged between her legs, putting delicious pressure on her core. She wasn't completely innocent. She knew how sex worked, and she had touched herself enough to know how to make herself feel good.

Beast chuckled against her neck, the sound dark and delicious. "Belle, stop." He grabbed her hip as she started to rock against his leg.

"Why?" she whined, not feeling even a little embarrassed.

"Because I'm not feeling nearly as gentlemanly as I should be."

Belle grabbed his hair and pulled his head back. His eyes glowed with his beast. "I don't want gentlemanly things."

He leaned down close, his hot breath skimming her cheek, her ear, before his teeth gently bit into her earlobe. "Do you really want your first time to be against a tree?" he whispered against her skin.

Shivers ran down her body, and she almost said yes, but reason won out. It was the middle of the day, and the castle wasn't far away. And no, she really didn't want her first time to be against a tree.

"That's what I thought." He pulled her close and kissed her neck again before setting her back on her feet and stepping back.

Beast ran a hand through his disheveled hair and looked at Belle. He had known she was fierce and brave, but he wouldn't have guessed she was that brazen, and he had to admit he liked it. Her kiss had surprised him, and her eagerness had almost made him forget himself. But she deserved more than a rough romp against a tree. He kept his eyes on Belle. Watched as she realized just what they had been doing. A blush ran up her neck and settled on her cheeks. She fisted her hands in her skirts, but he could see how they shook.

"Belle?"

She didn't look at him, and he stepped over and tilted her head up with a finger under her chin. "Belle?" He asked again once he caught her gaze. "Are you okay? Are we okay?"

More red stained her cheeks, but her lips pulled into a genuine smile. "Yeah, sorry." She covered her face with her hands but then laughed and looked back at him. "I can't believe I did that."

"I don't mind," Beast grinned at her. He wanted to pull her back into his embrace. He wanted to throw her over his shoulder and carry her off or just take her right against the tree, finish what they had started. Instead, he took a step back.

"We should go pack our things. There's no telling how long we will be gone."

"Yeah. And find me some pants." Belle smiled up at him again before turning and walking back towards the castle.

Beast washed his face in the cool water Potter had brought in. They had packed, looked over the maps again, ate dinner, and then looked at the maps some more. And for the first time since he had gotten home from his last hunt, Belle had bid him goodnight and walked to her own room.

He wanted to hurl the wash basin against the wall. Instead, he wiped his face while controlled anger made his fingers ache. He should have been smarter. Kept a tight hold of himself. But her kiss had taken him by complete surprise, and then everything had moved too far. He pulled his shirt off, not bothering with the buttons. The fabric tore under his hands, and once he started, he couldn't stop. He ripped the shirt apart, sending buttons and fabric flying.

"Beast?"

The soft voice stopped him, and he turned to face Belle. She stood just inside the door, her nightdress hiding her from neck to floor.

"You came."

"Was I not supposed to?" she asked, suddenly looking nervous.

"No, I mean, I prefer you here, with me. I just thought I had scared you away."

Belle looked up at him, one eyebrow raised. "Scared away?" she asked.

"Well, you do have a habit of running away." He stalked to her, backing her up until her back hit the door. He placed his hands on either side of her, caging her in.

"I'm not running now."

Beast pressed his lips against her neck and inhaled deeply, trying to calm his body down. He wanted to rip the ugly dress off her and claim her. Tell her that if she spent one more night in his bed, he would never allow her to walk away. Her scent had changed after her first shift, and the heady mix of woman and beast called to every part of him. He wanted to howl at the moon and sink his teeth deep into her, marking her as his.

"Ready for bed?"

Belle nodded against him, her breath hitching a little. Beast pushed back, grabbed her up, and carried her to the bed. He carefully tucked her under the covers before he crawled under them on what had become his side of the bed.

He leaned over her, looking down into her big brown eyes. She had been so bold outside the castle, caught up in passion. But lying here in the bed, a bit of fear shimmered in her eyes.

"Easy." He leaned down and kissed her. Claimed her mouth as he wanted to claim the rest of her. He grabbed her and rolled them, putting Belle on top.

"You're in control, beauty. I'm at your mercy."

Belle licked her lips and stared down at Beast. He

had placed his arms above his head, grabbing hold of the headboard. He stared at her with a heated gaze. She felt that gaze as it moved over her body, lighting a fire deep inside her. She trailed her fingers over his chest, felt the hard muscles and smooth skin until her fingertips stopped at the knotted skin of an old scar. She leaned down and kissed it. Beast shivered at her touch, and she couldn't help but smile. He was always in control. Of himself, of the situation. She figured that having lived so many years, there wasn't much he left to chance. But she wanted to break that control. She wanted to unleash what he had shown her a glimpse of outside before he pulled himself together.

Not that there weren't any nerves. Knowledge and her own fingers were not the same as practical experience. She acknowledged the fear and then let it go. This was Beast. He wouldn't hurt her. In fact, he had given her full control.

She looked up and met his gaze, his different-colored eyes glowing in the light from the single lamp burning near the washstand. She held his gaze as she leaned down and kissed another scar, her tongue trailing over his heated skin.

She closed her teeth over his nipple, biting down carefully. A delicious growl rumbled through him, gathering the heat in her body at her center. She wanted him. Wanted his touch, his taste, his everything.

She bit him harder and watched as his body shook.

"Belle."

She loved the way he growled her name. "Yes?" she looked up at him, feigning innocence.

"You're playing with fire." The headboard groaned under his fingers, but he never moved his hands.

"I like fire," Belle said and kissed down his stomach. She hesitated when she reached the edge of his pants. Was she really gonna do this? Her hands shook, and her breathing became erratic. Need burned through her but so did her nerves.

"Belle?"

She looked up at Beast. "I… I need…" She wasn't sure what she needed. To stop? To rip his clothes off? Beast let go of the headboard and sat up, cupping her face.

"Shhh, I got you. Just tell me what you need, and it's yours."

"You," she whispered. "I need you."

Beast growled low and pulled her into his lap, manhandling her until she was sitting with a leg on each side. Her nightdress was pushed up around her hips, and she felt him, hot and warm, through the thin fabric of his sleep pants. His fingers twisted in her hair, and Belle moaned when he pulled her head back, kissing her neck. He released her hair, but he never stopped kissing her bare skin. Her nightgown split under his hands, and then he leaned back, looking at her naked form.

"You're stunning, Beauty. I could feast on you for days."

Belle ran a hand down his chest. "Only a few days?"

He pulled her close, claiming her through his kiss, and Belle wrapped her hands in his hair, never wanting him to stop.

"I could feast on you forever," he said when he finally broke the kiss.

Belle was burning with need, and when his lips closed over one of her nipples, she nearly came undone. "Beast," she sighed and pushed herself closer to him. Her hips moved on their own, rubbing against him. His big hands grabbed her ass, fingers digging into her flesh, guiding her movements.

"That's it, take what you need from me," Beast said as Belle moaned against his neck. Heat swirled through her body, pooling at her core. Her breath came in small gasps, her fingers biting into his shoulders. She was coming undone, all that she was, ripping apart. She struggled to hold on to them, grasping at them so they couldn't float away.

"It's okay to let go, Beauty. I'll catch you."

Belle screamed as the pleasure spiraled, broke her apart, and threatened to carry her away. Beast's strong arms wrapped around her, catching her when she thought she would fall. Belle leaned against him, letting his strength protect her.

Beast carefully placed her on the bed, discarding what was left of the destroyed nightgown from her body.

"You think you can handle some more?" Beast whispered against her lips. Belle nodded, not sure if she was telling the truth or lying. Her mind was a jumbled mess, and still, she burned, wanting more, needing more. She gasped as his fingers trailed down between her breast, his lips following in a burning line.

A moan left her when his tongue trailed over her opening, swirling around the little bundle of pleasure she had spent so many nights touching. She was so sensitive. The pleasure was too much and not enough. One of her hands wrapped in his hair to keep him in place, or maybe pull him away, she wasn't sure.

"You're so fucking wet," Beast said and sat back, ripping at his pants. Belle watched as he tore them off, revealing every inch of delicious man. She wanted to touch every part of him. Lick and kiss every scar. Her gaze fell on his manhood.

"That's not gonna fit," she blurted, then blushed. She had used her fingers a few times. Two of them were enough to make her feel almost uncomfortable full.

Beast chuckled and grabbed her leg, kissing his way up the inside of her thigh. "I promise it'll fit." He kissed his way over her hip, up to her breasts. He licked and sucked them until Belle was panting again, begging for more. Then she felt him, hot and hard against her entrance. Her breath hitched, and she opened her eyes, staring up into Beast's blue and golden ones.

"Keep your eyes on me," Beast said. He leaned down and kissed her before pushing up on his knees, sitting between her knees. He grabbed her legs, opening her up more, his gaze never leaving hers.

It didn't hurt, not really. But the stretch burned, and she couldn't help the almost silent gasp. Beast stilled above her. "You okay?" he asked.

"Yeah," Belle panted. "Just go slow."

He released her legs and leaned down to kiss her. "We have all the time you need."

His fingers found her little bundle of pleasure, and

as he expertly played with it, her muscles started to relax again.

"That's it," he smiled at her and slid deeper. "Wrap your legs around me."

She did as told, and Beast slid as deep as he could, filling her completely. He slid back, and Belle moaned. It felt strange, but good, and his fingers helped stoke the fire inside her that had burned down to embers when he started to enter her. Their bodies came together in a dance of pleasure, and Belle was swept up in ecstasy as the fire roared inside her, threatening to burn her to ash.

Strong fingers grabbed her chin. "Beauty, I told you to keep those pretty eyes on me. I want to see you fly apart."

Belle opened her eyes, watched the muscles bunch and shift under Beast's skin, the sweat covering him in a glittering sheen. She wanted to taste him, but the pleasure was spiraling, threatening to destroy her. She moaned and gasped, fingers digging into Beast's thighs.

Beast growled, his rhythm faltering. She saw the moment his perfect control broke. Saw the beast in him take over. He leaned over her, resting his weight on one arm, the other pulling her leg up, opening her, changing the angle. His thrusts were almost brutal, every breath he took a growl, and Belle wanted it all. Her fingers ripped into his back, her hips meeting him move for move.

The pleasure finally ripped her apart, and she screamed as she flew into a million pieces. Beast wrapped his arms around her, pounding into her, and with a growl, he sank his teeth into her shoulder.

Beast lay on his back, Belle sprawled on top of him. She wasn't sleeping, he could feel her fingers exploring the scratches she had given him on his arms, but she wasn't completely awake either.

He gently touched the bite on her shoulder. He hadn't meant to do it. Hadn't meant to lose control like that, but there was something about her that just made him lose every shred of control.

"Are you okay?" he whispered in her ear. He should have been gentler for her first time, but she had seemed to enjoy every part of it.

"Mhmm," she breathed against his chest.

Beast cleared his throat. He didn't want to bring it up, but she truly had made him lose all control. "I didn't pull out."

Belle wriggled around a bit until she could look up at him. "Pull out?"

"I shouldn't have spilled inside you. I'm sorry."

Belle frowned at him before understanding widened her eyes. She pushed away from him, and Beast's heart skipped a beat. He wouldn't let her run. Not ever again. But she didn't run, didn't even more far, just lay on the bed beside him. She grabbed his hand and pulled him to his side before placing it on her stomach. The scar on her face was far from the only mark she had been left with that day fifteen years ago, and she used his fingers to trace a cluster of them running from under her ribs on one side to her thigh on the other.

"When the monster hurt me, the doctors weren't sure I would survive. It hadn't just ripped my skin. My insides were damaged too. They were surprised I even made it back to the city alive."

Back then, Beast had been surprised she had survived too. Now he knew she was the strongest woman he would ever meet.

"Some parts of me were so damaged they had to take them out. I was lucky. There's a healer in town who knew what to do."

She stopped his fingers at the worst part, where her skin was dipping and raising as if parts of her had been ripped away and the rest had been sewn together to cover the hole.

"I can't get children. I don't bleed. There's nothing left."

She looked up at him, and even in the darkness of the room, he could see her imploring eyes, asking if he would think less of her for something she had never had any control over.

"I'm sorry for what happened to you." He pulled her close, kissed her, and ensured the blankets covered her from head to toe.

He was nearly asleep when he heard her whisper, "I'm not." He tightened his grip on her and kissed the top of her head before sleep dragged him under.

Chapter 14

Belle rode a lovely gelding called Kalon. After meeting Beast's horses, Belle quickly realized that there was a distinct Greek theme in the way he named them.

The name fit the big horse, though, because he was just about the prettiest thing she had ever seen. Glossy black, long mane and tail and long white hair on his legs. He looked majestic.

"You okay?" Beast asked.

"Perfect," Belle said and gave him a quick smile. She wasn't quite used to sitting alone on the big animal and constantly feared she'd somehow slide off. That she was sore in certain places and sitting in the saddle made her a bit uncomfortable didn't help at all.

"Try to relax a bit more. It'll make your seat more natural, and you'll feel more secure."

Belle glared at Beast. She already knew that. Beast had given her lessons since they decided they needed to hunt the witch.

She wriggled her toes in her new boots. She had no idea how Beast had managed, but when she woke up that morning, not only did he have a stack of pants and shirts in her size waiting for her, but he also had found a pair of robust boots. She glanced at Beast. They were dressed identically, except Beast looked dangerous and capable.

Her gaze moved from his face down over his broad shoulders and further. A shiver ran through her as her thoughts returned to the night before. She had never felt so free, so beautiful. Need pooled in her in a rush of heed. She wanted to grab Beast and rip his clothes off. She wanted to do it all over again.

"If you keep looking at me like that, Beauty, I might have to finish what we started in the garden yesterday."

Belle ripped her gaze away from his thigh and met his amused eyes. But behind the humor, need and lust burned.

"Maybe I wouldn't mind that," she said and almost laughed when a low growl left Beast.

"Don't tempt me," he said and steered Agathon closer to her. He leaned down and claimed her lips, and Belle very much wanted to tempt him. But before she got the chance, he pulled away, cursing under his breath.

Belle reached out to grab him and pull him back but hissed when it pulled at the bite on her shoulder. She had hardly felt it last night and had been shocked when she saw it that morning in the mirror. Her shoulder wore a distinct bite, except it wasn't made by human teeth. The flesh around it was bruised, and the muscles hurt.

She had managed to keep how bad it was from Beast. He had been quite growly when he had woken her that morning, and he kept apologizing about it. Not that he shouldn't apologize for it, but she didn't want him to fuzz. He had already been worried about bringing her, and she had been worried he'd try and delay their trip. She didn't want that. There was a monster out there that needed to die before it destroyed some other girl's life.

"Belle, what's wrong?" Beast asked and stopped Agathon. Kalon dutifully followed the stallion's lead.

"Nothing," she tried but shut up when she met Beast's eyes. Anger burned in them, not at her, but at himself. "It's just a little sore. I'm fine, really."

"Belle, don't lie to me."

"Fine," she growled back, very much wanting to cross her arms in annoyance but knowing that would probably just hurt more. "It's itchy. My muscles all the way to my fingers hurt, and for some reason, it feels like the area is burning."

Beast jumped off Agathon and gently lifted her down from Kalon. He carefully undid the top buttons of her shirt and pulled it aside. "It's hurting because I pierced the muscle, and it's itching and burning because your accelerated healing has kicked in." He carefully traced the bite with a finger, and cold spread through her skin, chasing away the heat and the itching.

"What are you doing?" Belle asked and shivered from the cold.

"Once you learn to control the shift, you'll also learn to control other parts. For me, it's ice and snow. I suspect yours will be fire." He pulled his finger away and buttoned her shirt back up. Belle reached up with her good arm and touched his face, running her fingers over his jaw. "Thank you," she stood on her toes, and Beast bent down so she could give him a kiss. "Now, if you're done being all caveman, can we get back on the horses?" She asked and raised an eyebrow. Beast growled and pulled her closer, claiming her in a heated kiss.

When he let her go, she was panting and had no interest in getting back on the horse.

They rode for another hour before she felt compelled to break the silence. "Will you teach me how to fight?"

"I thought you already knew how to fight," he said with a straight face, and Belle suddenly felt the overwhelming need to punch him.

"Don't be mean."

"You really want to learn how to fight?"

"I'm wanted for being a witch, can shift into a monster, and we're on our way to hunt both a monster and a potential real witch. I think it would be irresponsible not to learn how to fight."

"In that case, yes, I'll teach you."

Belle relaxed. It had been one of the things she was nervous about. Sure she could throw a punch, but that didn't mean she had any survival skills when it came to a real fight. Something her encounter in town had proved to be lacking. She was still furious about that. She wished Beast had hurt them more. Wished she had had the ability to hurt them.

"What's going on? You suddenly look like you want to stab someone."

"Just thinking about the men in town." She looked

over and saw anger flash on Beast's face before it became carefully neutral.

"Anything specific?"

"I wished I had had the ability to hurt them like they wanted to hurt me."

"You did hurt them," Beast said.

"What are you talking about? All I did was panic."

"You decided their fate. I was simply the tool you used to hurt them."

Belle gaped at him. "You'd have done a lot worse. They deserved a lot worse."

Beast raised an eyebrow and stared at her. "Had I decided their fate, I'd have killed those men for touching you, Belle. But is that really what you wanted?"

Belle thought it over. She could have forgiven them for wanting to turn her in as a witch. Fear and hunger could make people do stupid things. She had witnessed that her whole life. But they hadn't just wanted to turn her over for money. They had wanted her. For that, they deserved a lot more than a knife through their hands. "Should have asked you to cut their cocks off," Belle said, her voice dripping with anger.

Beast finally seemed to come out of the funk he had been caught in all morning since he saw the bite and laughed. "Next time, tell me that."

Beast was stoking the fire when Belle wiped her

hands on her pants and stood.

"So, how are we going to do this?" She asked and looked at him expectantly.

"Do what?" He asked.

"Teach me how to fight."

Beast looked up at her and shook his head. "I'm not going to teach you before your shoulder is healed."

Belle glared at him. "We'll be hunting a monster within a week. How will I do that if you won't teach me?"

"I am hunting a monster within a week. You are going to stay back with the horses."

Anger clouded Belle's pretty face.

"Belle, even if we trained all day the next week, you will not be ready to go hunt a monster before you get your shift under control."

The fight left Belle, and she slumped back against the fallen tree they were using as cover against the wind.

"It's not working. I keep trying to do as you say. Relax and feel the beast within me. But I don't feel anything. Maybe I'm not really a beast."

Beast sat down beside her and pulled her into his arms. "Belle, I saw you. I got the scar to prove it." He pulled up his sleeve and showed her the white lines on his arm. It looked like they were years old when it had been only three weeks. He leaned down and kissed her. "And you're the most magnificent creature I have ever laid my eyes on. I don't know what is keeping you from connecting with your beast. Maybe it's because you weren't created like me. We still don't know why you've turned into a beast and not a monster. But I promise she's in there."

"The full moon is only a week away. What if I can't control her."

"I'll ensure we are far from everything when the full moon hits, and I'll shift too. I'm bigger, stronger, and in control. I'll keep you safe."

"It's not me I'm worried about."

"I know. I'll keep them safe too."

They sat in silence for a bit, and Beast thought she had fallen asleep when she suddenly asked in a small voice. "Can I see your beast?"

Beast froze. He had never let anyone see his beast. Not like this. But he wanted Belle to know him. All of him.

"You can if you promise not to run." He didn't want her afraid of him.

"I promise," she said and looked at him with an excited smile.

"Wait, what about the horses?" Belle asked.

"They know me. I've spent enough hours around them as my beast that they don't scare easily."

Beast stood and started to undress, and Belle's eyes went from excited to lust filled in a heartbeat.

"Are you sure you want me to shift?" he asked with a smirk.

"Yes," she said, but her gaze ate him up, making certain parts of Beast take notice. He did his best to ignore it and stepped into the shadows, away from the fire.

"The shift leaves me a bit confused and grumpy. So, just stay sitting where you are."

Belle nodded, and Beast closed his eyes. He called

his beast, and it broke free in tearing skin. For a heartbeat, he became pain. Blood coated his tongue, and then he stood on four legs. He shook from nose to tail, flinging off the tingling that lingered in his muscles. He blinked and looked around him. The world had shifted, become clearer. The shadows had lighted, letting him see details his human half couldn't. A sweet scent filled his nose, and he turned to the source. A small woman sat on the other side of the fire.

He stared at her, and she looked back with not an ounce of fear.

Mine, every part of his being screamed.

He stalked over, his paws almost soundless on the soft grass. The woman was sitting very still, a small smile on her lips.

"You are magnificent," she said, and knowledge floated back into his mind. Belle, his Beauty. He stopped and sat down, opening his mouth in a beastly grin.

Belle took it as permission and pushed up, walking closer. "You're so big. I think I could ride you." She reached out and ran her fingers through his fur, and Beast shuddered under her gentle touch.

"Am I as big as you?" She asked and stepped back from him, looking at him as if trying to imagine herself in her beast form.

Beast shook his head and stood, then bent his legs until his back was at the right height or at least the height he had estimated her to be. She hadn't exactly stood still for examinations.

Belle walked around him, and he stood frozen, still

half afraid he would scare her into running. Part of his beastly half laughed at that. They wouldn't mind a good chase.

Belle pulled at his front leg, and he dutifully lifted it. She ran her fingers over the paw and tapped each of his claws before she released him again.

Belle had never seen anything as amazing as Beast in his other form. He was almost as tall as Agathon and covered in shaggy fur. He was a mix of white and light grays, and she wanted to bury her face in it.

"Open," she said and tapped her finger against his mouth. She swore he rolled his eyes, and she couldn't help but smile. She examined him as one might do when buying a new steed, but she couldn't help it.

His teeth were as long as her fingers, and she had no doubt they could rip her apart with ease. The monster that had taken her all those years ago had done plenty of damage, and his face had been more human, his teeth smaller.

Beast closed his mouth, rumbled deep in his belly, and stepped back a few steps, and then the most magically thing happened. The long hairs on the back of his neck started to glow with a pale blue light. The light spread down his back until the tip of his tail glowed almost white. A gust of cold wind blew over her skin, dispelling the warmth, and frost started to spread in the grass around his paws.

137

Something stirred within Belle, and she gasped as it felt like claws pushed against her stomach from the inside. She buckled over, and Beast was there, naked and cold, holding her close in his arms.

"What's happening?" She gasped between waves of pain. Logically she knew what was happening, but she needed him to tell her she was wrong. It couldn't happen like this. The full moon was still a week away, and she wasn't ready. Cold hands touched her face, and she looked up into Beast's calm eyes.

"It's your beast. She wants to come out. Me shifting must have called to her."

Belle screamed as claws ripped into her chest from the wrong side.

"Easy. You need to stop fighting her and let her take over. I know you're scared, but I promise I'll make sure nothing happens."

Belle didn't think she had much choice. Her beast was coming out no matter what Belle did or wished for. "The horses," Belle gasped. It was her biggest fear. To hurt Beast's beloved horses.

"Are safe. Just let it happen."

The world tilted and filled with pain. White spots burst in her vision, blinding her, and then the world became clear.

Hunger burned in her stomach, and she whirled on the prey standing behind her.

"No," a voice said, deep and dark. *Dangerous,* her blood sang through her. she turned towards it.

"Remember, you're in control. Just give it a few seconds, and it'll all come back to you."

She looked into those mismatched eyes and felt

safe. Dangerous, but never to her.

Belle opened her mouth to ask what was happening, but all there came out was a growl and whine.

"Hehe, yeah, it takes a bit to get used to being unable to talk." Beast stepped closer and held out his hand.

Belle carefully extended her nose. His skin carried the scent of sun, leather, and horse. And under it was the scent of man and beast.

Beast moved his hand over her nose, and she pulled back, afraid she'd somehow hurt him.

"You won't hurt me." Beast extended his hand again, and this time Belle let him. She let out a purr as Beast ran his strong hands through her fur, rubbing behind one of her ears.

"Let's run," he said and stepped back. His human skin split and his beast spilled forth. He looked at her, yipped, and ran. Belle followed.

Chapter 15

Belle woke wrapped around Beast, both of them completely naked. She shivered against the morning damp and cold. Summer was coming to an end, and it would only be a few weeks until the nights would begin to be cold. Last night was a blur in her mind, and it didn't feel completely real. She had actually done it. She had shifted to her beast and stayed in control. There had been a few times when her beast tried to lead her astray, but Beast had been by her side, and with a few growls, he had gotten her back on track.

Belle tried to burrow closer to Beast, but the cold finally forced her to move. She sat up and grabbed for the blankets bunched around their feet. She twisted to cover them both with the blankets but stopped when her gaze fell on Beast's cock. She hadn't really seen it, not like this. The night they came together in bed, she had been too shy to really explore it. And while she'd seen him naked, she'd tried not to stare.

Her gaze flicked up to his face, but he was still asleep. She looked back down. She wanted to reach out and touch, but would that be okay? She thought back to the things he had said and done. The way he looked at her. Carefully she reached out and traced a finger down the length of him. The cock jumped under her touch and grew bigger, and she snatched her hand back.

"Don't stop."

Her gaze jerked up and met Beast's half-lidded gaze, watching her with lust and need. She kept looking at him as she reached out and ran her finger over him again. Beast gasped at the contact, and she felt her confidence grow. She carefully wrapped her fingers around it and felt the flesh harden within her grip. She traced her thumb up and down but wasn't quite sure what would be okay to do. What would feel good, and what would hurt?

"Can you show me?" she asked. She released her grip, wanting him to take over, but instead, he grabbed her hand. He wrapped her fingers back around him and then wrapped his own hand around hers.

"I like some pressure like this, and then move your hand up and down."

He started to move their hands, and Belle felt the soft slide of skin against her palm. She tore her gaze from their joined hands when Beast moaned. He was still watching her, and she felt heat pool in her core at the need burning in his eyes. She leaned over him, claiming him with a kiss. His free hand tangled in her hair, but he let her keep control of the kiss.

"A little faster," Beast moaned against her lips, and she realized that at some point, he had let go of her hand, letting her back in control. She did as he asked, feeling powerful, controlling his pleasure. Beast swore and buried his head against her neck, kissing her heated skin. She felt dampness between her legs, and her pussy clenched thinking about taking him inside.

"Belle, stop, or I'm gonna come."

But Belle didn't want to stop. She wanted to be the one to bring him this pleasure, and she wanted to watch him as she did. She pulled his hair, and he leaned back, looking at her. His face was flushed, and the muscles in his jaw and neck were tensed up.

"I want to watch," she said, and Beast swore again before another moan left him. Her gaze shifted between watching him and her hand. His hips jerked, and he threw his head back. "Fuck, Beauty," he growled, and pleasure tightened his face as his eyes lighted with the beast. He grabbed her hair and pulled her down into a searing kiss. His cock jerked in her grip, and she felt wetness drip over her fingers.

He grabbed her hand and pulled it off him, and she watched, fascinated, as he swiped her fingers through the seed he had spilled all over his stomach. He watched her with a heated gaze and held her fingers to her lips. She was panting, need burning through her, and his look only fueled her fire. She held his eyes as she carefully licked over her fingers. The salty taste of him filled her mouth, and when she sucked her fingers into her mouth, Beast growled and grabbed her shoulders. The world tilted, and she stared up into Beast's face.

"One day, Beauty, I want you to suck on my cock, just like that."

Belle gasped as her pussy clenched at the idea.

"But for now, I'll take care of you." Beast kissed

down her chest, licking over her nipples. His fingers circled her pussy, teasing that bundle of pleasure, making her push up against his hand. She wanted him inside her, and she didn't much care if it was his fingers or his cock that filled her up.

Beast bit down on her nipple as he pushed two fingers into her, and Belle gasped at the dual sensations. It felt so good and so full.

"Fuck, Beauty, you're so tight and wet."

He moved his attention to her other breast, and it felt like there was a straight connection between every place he touched and her pussy. She panted and moaned, her fingers buried in his hair.

With a growl, Beast grabbed her legs. He spread her open and swallowed her scream as he pushed inside her. She was so full, and everything burned and stretched, and she wanted more.

She ripped herself free from his kiss and bit his ear before ordering him to move. Their panting, moaning, and growling mixed into a song of pleasure, as Beast took her in hard thrusts.

She flew apart when the fire roared inside her, and Beast echoed her scream with a growl.

They lay on their sides, looking at each other, both trying to get their breathing back under control.

"Now that's what I call a 'good morning'," Beast said, and Belle couldn't help but laugh. She felt free and relaxed.

"I was just curious," she felt the heat in her cheeks and knew it was silly after what they had just done, but there was no helping it.

"Beauty, I'm not complaining. You can explore as much as you want." He kissed her, and Belle melted into it.

"Why do you call me that?"

"Call you what?"

"Beauty."

"Because when you're caught in pleasure, you're the most beautiful thing I've ever seen," Beast said before pushing to his feet. Belle watched him walk to the small creek the horses were tied by. She followed the lines of his body, marveling that she had a right to every part of him. He made her feel beautiful.

He stepped into the shallow water and knelt down, washing the evidence of their coming together away from his body. Belle realized she felt quite sticky too. Maybe a quick dip wouldn't be a bad idea.

She gasped as the cold water swirled around her feet but still knelt down, her knees sinking into the soft sand. She quickly washed, scrubbing every inch of her, and when she stepped out of the water again, Beast was already dressed. She hurried into her clothes, not caring that they clung to her wet body. She was pulling on her shirt when Beast stopped her.

"Let me see the wound." He carefully ran his fingers over it, but there was no lingering pain or heat.

"It feels okay." She said.

"It's almost completely healed. Probably because of the shift last night. Going from one form to another speeds up the healing process."

He released her, and she buttoned up her shirt. What she really wanted to do was rip it all off again and do wicked things with Beast until she needed another bath. She had no idea where this need came from, but it burned through her. She ignored it and took the apple Beast offered her. As much as she enjoyed the things they did together, they did have a monster to kill.

Beast kept a sharp eye on Belle throughout the day. The full moon was only six days away, and she was clearly feeling the effect. The moon's call kept the beast just under their skins. Beast felt it too, but he had learned to control it. Not that he was completely unaffected, and sometimes he fell into the trap too. Still, for Belle, everything was new, and she was clearly having a hard time. It was always a dangerous time. The beast within them would use any excuse to break free.

Belle's eyes were glowing with her beast, and she was almost bouncing on Kalon with unused energy. It was lucky the horse was so good-natured, or he might have tried to throw her. A herd of deer broke out of the tree line, and Belle focused on them with a predatory glint.

"Belle," Beast called, but she didn't react. He swore under his breath and steered Agathon in front of her. "Belle, focus," he snapped and caught her gaze as she tried to follow the deers' movements.

Instead of Belle getting back in control, she snarled

at him. Beast snarled back, the sound rumbling in his chest. "Belle, I swear that if you don't get back in control right now, I'll tie you down and spank you." He wasn't quite sure why he had said that to her, but the image it conjured in his mind made his cock twitch.

Belle blinked, and the unmistakable scent of lust wafted from her. Apparently, Belle liked that idea too.

She cleared her throat and shifted a little in the saddle. "Sorry, I didn't mean to growl at you."

"It's okay. It's the moon calling to you. You'll learn to get it under control."

"Or you'll spank me?" she asked, her mouth pulling into a grin.

"Don't tempt me," he said, turning Agathon around so they could keep riding.

They had made camp at the foot of some giant boulders sticking out of the ground. A small forest lake spread out beside them, and both he and Belle had washed in it while their dinner cooked. Belle had asked him to teach her to fight again, but he refused. With the beast riding her so close, it was too dangerous. Instead, he'd offered to teach her to use the bow. She had agreed, and they had spent an hour shooting at an old half-rotten tree stump. It had finally gotten too dark, and Beast had unpacked their blankets. Now they sat close together, watching the fire slowly dying down.

"You said you were a soldier. Will you tell me about it?"

"What would you like to know?" he asked after a

bit of hesitation. He wasn't used to anyone wanting to know anything about his life. He had lived alone with only the few servants at the castle for so long. And they knew better than to ask him personal questions.

"What wars did you fight in?"

"As many as I could. It seems humans always have one reason or another to kill each other. When one war stopped, I simply moved on to the next."

"But you were fifteen."

"Fifteen-year-olds are forced into wars all the time."

"Which war was your first?"

"The war between the Karelian Kingdom and the state of Awester."

"Awester?" Belle asked.

"It was a small part of the Karelian kingdom. But they wanted to break free. The king of Karelian didn't agree."

"What happened?" she asked.

"The Karelian kingdom had overwhelming forces, but we were fighting people on their land. Mountains and forests like here. It took almost a year before Awester was completely destroyed." He didn't remember much about that year. He had been so consumed with anger that he constantly fought his beast.

"How did you get the name Beast?"

"I joined a group of mercenaries. Most armies didn't much like hiring outsiders, but the mercenaries I joined were well known."

"Mercenaries. That's men who fight for money, right?"

"Yes. So I joined up with them, and we went where ever the fighting was the worst. It didn't take long before I earned the name Beast among the other mercenaries."

"Why?"

Beast hesitated. "Because they said only a beast could kill so many men in a single day." He glanced at Belle. He worried she might be disgusted by his past, but she was watching the fire looking relaxed and content.

"Why did you stop fighting?"

"The winter rebellion," Beast said. Of all the battles he had been part of, that one was his biggest regret.

"That was in one of the southern kingdoms, right?" Belle asked.

"You've heard about it?"

"Not much. Just that the people rebelled against their king."

"Yeah. A bad summer had destroyed the harvest, and people were starving." Beast hadn't known what he was getting involved in. Hadn't much cared either. When the rebellion ended three months later, he had put his sword away, taken his horse, and gone home. Killing armed soldiers was one thing, but the Winter rebellion had been a slaughter. Starved people armed with rocks and farm tools fighting because their children were dying.

Belle hugged him close, and he took comfort in her embrace. They sat like that, letting the darkness and the dying embers wrap them in the quiet of the night.

"Do you really not remember your name?" Belle whispered.

"I do, but the name belongs to a boy who died in that garden when he was fifteen," Beast said. Belle opened her mouth, but he put a finger over her lips before she could speak.

"Don't ask. I'm not him, not anymore. I've been Beast for a very long time."

Belle stared into his eyes, and he could see so many questions lingering. Questions he couldn't and wouldn't answer. Not even for her.

Finally, she nodded and leaned back against his side.

"Tell me a story," she said.

Beast smiled and started on one of the many tales he had lived through.

Chapter 16

They had been traveling another four days, and the full moon was only a day away. Belle found it harder and harder to keep her mind straight. She could be having a conversation with Beast, and suddenly something would grab her attention, and she had to use every ounce of control not to let her beast break free.

She looked at Beast and felt heat in her cheeks. A bruise covered the right side of his jaw. They had been packing up their camp when she caught the scent of rabbits. She had taken off after them, and Beast had tried to stop her. She had punched him before she even realized what she was doing. Beast had answered with a growl and tackled her. Then her beast had been distracted by a whole other set of thoughts. She had to mend his shirt when they broke for the night.

The wind shifted, and a sour stench hit her. Kalon danced under her, and Beast swore under his breath.

"Stay here," Beast said and turned Agathon. The big stallion took off with thundering hoofs, and Belle stared after him. Did he really think she was going to just stay back? With an annoyed snarl, she sent Kalon after him. She wasn't nearly as good a rider as Beast, but Kalon was eager to run, and her new enhanced strength let her stay on top, even if she was sure she didn't look pretty while doing it.

She pulled Kalon to a stop when she spotted Agathon. She looked around and spotted Beast kneeling next to something on the ground. He didn't look up at her, but he knew she was there.

"I didn't want you to see this," he said.

Belle jumped from Kalon's back and walked over to Beast. The sour stench was almost choking her, and she wasn't sure she wanted to see whatever was hiding halfway under the bush, either. She pulled in a sharp breath when she got close enough to see. It was a woman, or what was left of a woman. Her stomach was ripped open, and something had eaten the flesh of her thigh and chest. Long claw marks covered the rest.

She fought down the nausea that threatened to make her vomit up her breakfast. "The monster is here," she forced out.

"The kill is maybe half a day old. But it probably hasn't gone too far." Beast stood back up, and Belle fought to pull her eyes away from the woman. A small part of her looked at her and saw an easy meal.

"Belle?"

Belle didn't answer, just turned and puked. Beast swore behind her, then a cool hand was placed against her head, and her hair pulled back.

"I told you to stay back," Beast said. Belle took the offered water flask and cleaned her mouth before she turned to look at him, keeping her gaze firmly on him and off the body.

"I'm not a child, Beast," she growled.

Beast raised an eyebrow. "I know, but you are

151

newly turned and not used to seeing dead bodies, I presume."

Belle swallowed, still not looking at the body. "Yeah, well, I have to learn at some point."

"You don't have to," Beast said, but his tone said he already knew Belle wouldn't go away.

"I do. If I'm not one of the monsters, then I have an obligation to use my new powers to help stop them."

Beast nodded and turned back to the body. "What do you see?"

Belle tried looking at it again, but instead of seeing it as a person, she tried to look at the individual parts. The clues. She frowned as something hit her. "Why was she out here all alone?"

"She wasn't." Beast's face was hard, and the air around him was noticeably colder.

Belle looked at him sharply.

"What do you smell?"

Belle didn't want to take another deep breath, but she did want to learn. She drew in the air and coughed at the overwhelming stench.

"Try again."

She did and tried to get anything other than death.

"Let your beast help you."

Belle shifted through the smells. She knew rabbit and the soft scent of crushed pine needles. The sharp stench of predator made her growl, and Beast grabbed her arm when her whole body rocked forward, wanting to chase down that sick smell.

"Easy. No running off to hunt monsters."

Belle locked her muscles and tried to sift through all the smells in the air. So many of them were unknowns, but there, faintly, something familiar. She opened her eyes and looked at Beast with big eyes. She knew that scent, and before Beast could stop her, she sprinted around the bushes and deeper into the forest.

She didn't have to run far before she stumbled into a small clearing. A small stream cut through the clearing, and three colorful wagons stood in a semi-circle. Tears streamed down her cheeks as she took in the carnage. Everyone was dead. Marie, Phillipe, Nicolas, Emilie. All of them killed by the monster.

Beast came crashing into the clearing, pulling the horses. She threw herself into his body and sobbed against his chest. She didn't know why it hit her so hard. She didn't even know these people. But they helped her when she needed help. Had taken her in, clothed, and fed her despite her being a stranger. It was a kindness few had ever shown her.

Beast wrapped his arms around her and held her close, letting her cry out her sadness until only anger was left.

"Did you know them?" Beast asked when she finally stepped out of his embrace.

"They helped me when I ran from you. They were really nice." Her words were more growl than human speech, and her beast was howling to get out. She wanted to rip that monster apart. Hurt it for what it had done.

"I'm sorry," Beast said and took hold of her hand. It was a comforting gesture, but it also allowed him to keep control should her's fail. She recognized all this and was grateful for it.

"We should bury them," Belle said.

Beast wished he could agree. He wanted to do whatever it took to take that pain out of her eyes. "It's too dangerous. The monster fed and has probably found somewhere to hide. But it'll come back, and we can't afford to be tired from digging when it does."

Belle looked around the clearing, her face hardening the more she looked. "Let's burn them, then." Beast opened his mouth to protest, but in the end, he just nodded. She needed this, and even knowing that the smell of fire could send the monster running, he would give it to her.

Belle searched the wagons and found enough blankets to wrap the dead. He kept a sharp eye on her as they carefully started to pick up the bodies and carry them to the nearest wagon. She was so high-strung on emotions that there was no way of predicting what could happen. Worst case scenario was her losing complete control, shifting, and trying to feast on the dead. Though with the anger and sadness wafting off her, it was more likely she would shift and go after the monster. Beast completely understood her but running blindly after a monster was a good way to get hurt or killed. Even for a beast.

Belle placed the last body in the wagon, and Beast pushed the other two further away to prevent the fire from spreading. The oxen that had pulled the wagons were nowhere to be seen, and Beast figured they had run off when the monster attacked.

Beast opened a few oil lamps and poured the content all over the wagon floor and the bodies. Belle grabbed a still-burning oil lamp from one of the other wagons and coaxed the flame onto some kindle before tossing the whole thing into the wagon. They stepped back and watched as the flames devoured the wagon and the dead inside.

Belle took a deep breath and started to sing. It was a simple tune, and Beast had heard it enough that he could join in after a few words. They watched and sang, and Belle cried. Power started to stream from her, and the fire roared and grew in strength. The wood fell apart, turning to ash when the fire touched it. Beast wasn't even sure Belle knew what she was doing.

With the aid of Belle's powers, the wagon and the bodies were nothing but a smoldering pile of embers and ash before the end of an hour. Beast called his own powers and killed the last heat, ensuring nothing was left to burn down the forest.

Belle didn't say anything, just stumbled to the horses, and Beast lifted her onto Agathon's back. She didn't react when he sat behind her, simply leaned against him and closed her eyes.

He only rode far enough to escape the stench of death and fire before he stopped to make camp. If the monster was in the area, they might as well wait. It would come to them soon enough. They always did. Driven by pure instinct, they couldn't accept another predator near.

Belle seemed almost numb, and Beast let her sit on the forest floor, a blanket around her shoulders, while he built a fire and pulled out the last of their provisions. The cheese was still good, but the bread had gone quite stale. They'd need to visit a town soon, and on any other night, he would have gone hunting, but he wasn't gonna leave Belle alone.

"Belle, you need to eat something." Beast knelt in front of her and cupped the side of her head. She blinked and looked at him, and Beast gave her a small smile. He wished she hadn't seen the things she had today, but as she had pointed out, she wasn't a kid, and if he was honest, Belle had survived horrors already. She had earned her right to make her own decisions, even if he didn't always like them.

"Thank you," she said and took the food from him. She nibbled on the bread, and Beast made their blankets ready for sleep. It was still fairly early in the day, but the monster was likely to come out when darkness fell, and Beast would prefer to get a few hours of sleep before that. Once the fire was going strong, and Belle was tugged in, he checked the horses before joining her.

"I'm sorry," Belle said and buried her face against his chest.

"For what?" he asked back.

"For being so crazy," she grumbled against him, her words muffled against his shirt.

"You aren't crazy. It was just a bad situation."

"You didn't go all numb or anything."

"Do we really have to talk about my age again? You're gonna make me feel old."

Belle snorted, and Beast relaxed a bit. If she could find humor in his stupid words, then she would be just fine.

Belle looked up at him. "You aren't old."

Beast raised an eyebrow. He was old. Probably too old to even think about spending his life with someone as young as Belle.

"Okay, in years, you're old. But you aren't, like, old like my dad."

Beast laughed. "Thanks, that make me feel better."

Belle blushed. "I didn't mean it like that. I just mean that he was old here." She touched his chest. "And here." She ran a hand over his forehead. "You aren't. I sometimes forget just how much you must have seen and experienced." She stretched and kissed him, and he happily returned it.

Chapter 17

The moon hung big and heavy in the sky. One more day and it would be full. Belle shook her hands to try and dispel some of the energy coursing through her. In theory, she had understood that the magic that let them shift from human to beast was drawn by the moon, but she hadn't quite understood what that actually meant. Standing here under the moon, the call was so strong that the hair on her arms stood up as if reaching for the glowing orb in the sky.

They had only slept a few hours before Beast had shaken her awake. The fire had burned down, and Beast had quickly packed away their belongings.

"What are you doing?" she asked as she saw Beast releasing both horses from their bindings, slapping their rumps, and sending them running into the forest.

"The monster will smell us and ignore the horses. If we keep them here, they might get caught up in the fight."

"But how are we gonna travel if our horses are gone?" Belle asked while trying to ignore the fact that he had just said the monster would hunt them. They had always been the hunters in her head, and she didn't much like thinking of herself as prey.

"They won't go far, and I can always call them back."

Beast pulled her into a heated kiss, and Belle melted against him. She hadn't been blind to the fact that the closer to the full moon they came, the more heated everything became between them. As with every other emotion running in her body, she figured it was their beasts playing up. She was sure Beast knew the answer, but she was too embarrassed to ask.

"You need to shift," Beast said when he released her.

"Are you going to shift?"

"Yes. We heal faster and are stronger in human form, but we can still be broken. Our beasts are a lot more durable."

Belle wasn't sure if it was a good idea. With the moon calling, there was too high a risk she would lose control. She shook her head. Tomorrow she wouldn't have a choice anyway. Might as well get used to it.

She stripped off her clothes, and Beast picked them up and tossed them over a few branches in a tree. She let her gaze run over his naked form one last time, closed her eyes, and let her beast out. When she opened her eyes again, Beast stood in his beastly form. She gave him a wolfish grin. She had done it. Shifted and stayed herself. Beast gave her a lick on the nose and bumped his shoulder into hers before he started in between the trees, towards the traveler camp. Belle followed, her paws almost soundless despite her size.

As they got near the camp, the smell of death and smoke got stronger, but it was the stench of predator that made her hackles rise. She had gotten a faint trace of it in her human form, but now it made every hair stand up. It smelled wrong, sick. Beast nudged her side and gave her a pointed look, and she stopped her growling. It wouldn't do for them to scare away the monster when they were supposed to kill it.

A low bellow from an animal in pain sounded between the trees. Beast whirled at her, growled low, and gave her a look that said 'stay.'

Belle showed him her teeth, and when he ran off, she followed right behind. He might be the better fighter, but she wasn't a fragile human, and there was no way she would let him run into danger alone. He had been alone for too long. But no more.

Belle skidded to a stop. A monster stood before them, blood dripping from its monstrous face. It was a misshapen thing caught halfway between man and beast. One arm looked strong and powerful. It ended in something more paw than hand, and wicked claws tipped each finger stub. The other arm was longer and thinner, but so were the claws, which looked like thin blades at the end of each deformed finger. Dark gray fur covered patches of its body, while the rest was sagging human skin. The monster stood on two legs, its back hunched, and its human eyes glowed with madness.

The smell clogged her nose, and she was suddenly a little girl again, trying to protect her sister from the monster.

Beast kept himself firmly between Belle and the monster. She had barreled in after him but had come to a crashing stop on the other side of the brush. He could smell fear spiking off her, but he didn't dare give her a glance. While he was bigger than a monster and had more control, the monsters were driven by rage and blood lust. Things like pain and fear didn't deter them.

The monster screeched at them and put a leg on the still-twitching ox. Beast roared back. Normally he would circle the monster, trying to find a weak spot, but if he moved, he left Belle completely open. He cursed her in his head for refusing to listen and, at the same time, approved of her courage. Everything was so new for her, and she just threw herself into it.

The monster twisted and attacked, and Beast met it head-on. Claws ripped into his side as warm blood filled his mouth. His jaws were locked on the monster's arm, and he twisted his head, hearing the satisfying crack of bone breaking. The monster roared but kept clawing him, and Beast used his heavier bulk and rolled them on the ground. The monster kicked his side, and Beast used his paws to claw into its soft belly. They rolled and twisted in a whirl of claws and teeth. Blood flowed, filling the air with its coppery scent. Another snarl joined his, and the monster was flung away. He rolled his paws and saw Belle pacing back and forth in front of him, her fur glowing like fire, her paws burning the grass beneath them.

The monster roared, and Belle growled back, her hackles raised and her ears pinned. Beast walked to her side and gave her a soft nip on her shoulder as thanks.

They circled the monster, pacing each their way, forcing it to try and keep them both in its vision. With a snarl, it went for Beast again. He was wounded, and the scent of fresh blood drew it in. Belle's jaws clamped on its shoulder, crunching bones and ripping flesh. Beast jumped forward and bit into its other side. The monster roared, and Beast could do nothing as it clamped its teeth onto Belle's snout. She yipped but didn't let go. Beast growled and released his hold. With a twist of his body, he crushed the monster's throat between his teeth. The monster still fought them, too maddened to realize it was dying, and only when there was no more air in its body did it crumble to the ground.

Belle backed away and gently rubbed her snout with her paw. Blood flowed freely from the bite, along with a few gashed in the fur on her shoulders. Beast was bleeding from multiple cuts, and his body was starting to realize it had been in a fight. He walked to the monster and planted his massive paws on the monster's chest. He bit into the head and ripped it off, throwing it into the underbrush.

He limped to Belle and licked the wound on her face. She pulled away and growled at him, and he pinned his ears back. They stared at each other for a few heartbeats before Belle, with a huff, turned away and started to walk back to camp.

As soon as they reached camp, Belle started to shift back. Beast waited til she was human before he shifted back as well. Pain fired through his nerves, and he heard Belle softly curse under her breath as she flexed her fingers. Shifting when hurt sucked. There was no other word for it.

She was bleeding from wounds on her thigh and her ribs. Her nose was crooked, and bites covered her cheek and the tip of her nose. The wounds were already healing, but the nose would need to be set. He ignored his own wounds, blood flowing from his chest and shoulder, and walked to her.

"Belle," he said and stopped before he got too close. The full moon was less than a day away and shifting while hurt could bring the beast close to the surface.

She looked up at him and smiled. "Did you see me? I was awesome." She laughed and then winced when it pulled in her wounds.

"You were amazing. But I better set that nose before it heals wrong."

She touched it as if she hadn't noticed it was crooked and winced. He made her sit and sat behind her, cradling her between his legs. He pulled her back against his chest and put his thumbs against her nose. "Sorry," he said and pushed.

She growled and snapped her teeth. Tears started streaming down her face, and he kissed them away, tasting her blood on his tongue.

"Let's get the blood washed off. Then we can see if any of the wounds need help healing." He tried to stand, but Belle wrapped her hands in his hair and kept him behind her. She turned towards him. Kneeling between his legs, she pulled him close and kissed him. Tears still streamed from her eyes, but she claimed his mouth as if she was starving. He wrapped his arms around her and pulled her into his lap. The heady scent of blood, the victory in battle, and feeling her naked form slide against him sent spikes of need through him.

Belle pulled at his hair, and he leaned back so he could look into her eyes.

"I need you," she panted against his lips.

"I'm all yours," he said.

Beast groaned as she slid down his cock, taking him deep. He cupped her ass, and blood made his fingers slide against her skin. A small part of his brain said he should stop this. Get her cleaned up and check her wounds. But the biggest part wanted to stake his claim. He wanted to fuck her hard and sink his teeth into her flesh, making sure everyone knew that this warrior maiden was his.

He growled when she started rolling her hips, and he dipped his head and licked across her breast. The taste of Belle and blood exploded over his senses, and he bit into her flesh. She threw her head back and moaned loudly, and it was a fight not to pierce her skin. He pulled back, knowing he left bruises and not caring.

"Fuck, Beauty, I just want to mark every inch of you," he groaned and dug his fingers deeper into her flesh, controlling her rhythm, her speed.

Belle growled in response and he roared as her teeth pierced his neck, sending drops of blood rolling down his skin and mingling with the rest. She looked up at him, a drop of his blood clinging to her lips, and he grabbed her head and pulled her close, claiming her in a brutal kiss.

The moon called them both, claiming her price, and they paid it in pleasure, pain, and blood spilled.

He rolled them, putting Belle beneath him, and he used his fingers to send her over the edge, using her slick and their mingled blood to make his fingers slip over the little bundle of nerves. She came with a scream, her nails digging into his arms.

"Give me one more," he growled as he pounded into her, his fingers coaching another orgasm from her. His teeth pierced her skin just above her right breast, her hot blood flowing freely, sending him over the edge. He roared his release at the moon before rolling them both, so he could cradle her against his side.

"That's my Beauty." He kissed her gently, running his hand up and down her side. Blood streaked her skin, and she was shaking against him.

He forced himself to stand, still holding her in his arms, carried her to the stream's edge, and stepped into the cold water. It flowed red around them, and Beast carefully washed the blood from Belle. Her fingers moved gently over his skin, tracing wounds and marks.

"How's the nose?" he asked. They were lying under the blankets. He hadn't lighted another fire, and the chill of the night was touching their bodies. They really should have put on some clothes, but none of them wanted to lose the feel of the other.

"Sore," she said against his shoulder. She was tracing the bite she had given him with a finger, and every time she touched it, shivers ran through him.

"It'll be better with some sleep and food."

"I don't care about my nose," she said, and Beast kissed the top of her head.

"What happened when we saw the monster?" he asked.

"Just bad memories," she said and snuggled closer.

"Wanna talk about it?"

"No, not really. I just wanna sleep."

"Okay. Goodnight, Beauty."

"Goodnight."

Beast woke to nails digging into his flesh. Belle was whimpering in his arms, caught in another nightmare. She hadn't had any for a couple of weeks, but the day's event must have brought them back. He held her close and murmured silly things in her ears until she calmed again. If only her inner demons were as easy to slay as the monster.

Chapter 18

The full moon had come and gone, and they were only a few days from the town and castle that had been the home of one of the lost princes.

They had crossed the border into another kingdom the day before, and Belle felt very far from home. It had been a month since she left her village. A month of everything changing and being turned upside down. She looked at Beast riding beside her. She wasn't sure what would have happened if he hadn't come into her life. Would she have lived as an outcast in the tiny village for the rest of her life? Or would her beast have demanded to come out at some point? The thought of being trapped in that place, living her whole life without experiencing anything, made her shudder.

"Anything wrong?" Beast asked.

"Just thinking how my life would have been if you hadn't taken me away."

"How do you think it would have been?" Beast asked.

"Horrible," she said as her thoughts strayed to Gaston. Not only was she hated and feared in the village, but she had no doubt that Gaston would have found a way to get what he wanted from her. She wished she would meet him again. Then she would show him what happened when he touched what he had no right to touch. Maybe she and Beast could travel that way one day. She glanced back at Beast and smiled at the thought of what he would do to Gaston if he ever touched her.

"Then what have you smiling?"

"Revenge."

"Revenge?"

"Some people in this world deserve to be punished."

"Anyone in particular?"

Belle hesitated, but she wanted Beast to know. "Gaston," she finally said.

"Gaston?"

"A man back in town. All the girls want him because he's a skilled hunter and very handsome. Unfortunately, he's rotting on the inside."

"All the girls?" Beast asked, the beginning of a growl in his voice.

Belle rolled her eyes. "Don't worry. I kept him as far away as I could." She smiled a bit. "I broke his nose once."

Beast's voice had lost the teasing edge when he asked, "Why?"

Belle frowned at him. He had no reason to care that she had broken Gaston's nose, so where was the hard edge in his voice coming from? "Because his papa forgot to teach him manners."

"And you can't wait to break his nose again," Beast growled.

Belle blinked, confused. She had no idea what was

going on until realization hit her. That's what she said to Gaston while tied to the pole. "You were there the whole time," she said.

"I wish I could have gotten you out before he laid as much as a finger on you."

"You got me out. Without you, I'd have burned at the stake." She reached over and grabbed his hand.

"I'm not sure you can."

"Can what?"

"Burn at the stake. You walked out of your father's house without a single mark."

Belle swallowed. "Whatever their choice of killing me, I'm happy you got me out."

He gave her a sly smile. "You say that now."

"Hey, I was scared and confused, and some strange immortal man stole me away."

"I didn't steal you away. I saved you."

"You kidnapped me with the intent of killing me if I turned into a monster."

"Fine, I was saving everyone else. Happy?"

Belle laughed. She should be mad at him still. But she had seen what a monster could do. Bore both old and new scars from them. She was grateful someone was willing to hunt them down.

"Besides," Beast said. "You're not a prisoner anymore."

Belle smiled her sweetest smile at him. "So, if I was to leave right now, you'd let me?" She gasped as Beast grabbed her around the waist, hauling her out of Kalon's saddle and onto his. He grabbed her face with one hand, holding her in place with the other arm around her waist.

169

"I'm not gonna keep you against your will, Belle. But make sure you leave because you want to go and not because you're running just because you're scared." His gaze was intense, and Belle felt trapped in it. She reached up and pulled him down, her lips feather light against his.

"I promise, no more running." She kissed him, savoring the taste of man. Of him. The all-consuming need that made it feel like she couldn't breathe without him had lessened with the moon's waning, but she still wanted him all the time. Every look, every touch, made her whole body vibrate with need.

He ran his fingers over the bite on her shoulder, and she shuddered under his caress. Knowing she carried his mark just like he carried hers made her core clench.

"Most men will look at you and think you're no threat. But you're not human anymore, Belle. You're getting stronger and faster every day. Use it to your advantage." Beast grabbed Belle's arm slowly. Belle hesitated, then pretended to hit his elbow while twisting in his grip. He let her go.

"Good. Again."

He hadn't realized how much it had worried her that the men in town had so easily taken her hostage. But it was the first thing she had asked him to show her. How to get away if someone grabbed her.

Beast turned Belle around and wrapped his arms

around her. In a fight against him, her size was a disadvantage, but against a regular human being, her strength would offset any disadvantage her height might bring her.

"Now, what do you do if someone grabs you like this?"

Belle tried to muscle her way out, but Beast tightened his grip, keeping her close to his chest. After a minute, she finally stopped breathing hard.

"Thrashing around won't help you. Instead, lift your legs up. One of two things will happen. Your attacker will drop you because he's suddenly holding your full weight. In that case, you roll away, get up and run, or turn and attack. The other thing that can happen is that he carries your weight. In that case, you draw your legs up high, then kick back as hard as you can."

"What if I don't want to get free?" she asked, leaning into his chest instead of trying to escape him.

"Then I guess he gets to have some fun." Beast leaned down and kissed the side of her neck. Belle rubbed against him, and Beast nipped at her skin. With a curse, he stumbled back when pain exploded in his stomach and foot. Belle whirled around and backed away, a smirk firmly on her kissable lips.

"Guess I win," she said, still backing away.

Beast straightened, breathing deep to dispel the pain where her elbow had caught him. That little minx. Using her body to distract him. He had to give it to her; she was a savage little thing.

He looked at her, letting his beast fill his eyes. She had learned to control her shift, but Beast had spent hundreds of years controlling every part of his curse. Belle stopped smirking and took a few quick steps back, bringing her past the edge of the light cast from the fire and into the shadows between the trees. She blew him a kiss and ran.

He laughed, gave chase, and followed her in a crazy dash through the darkness. She was fast, and her smaller size let her turn fast, but Beast finally managed to catch up, his longer legs lending him extra speed. He grabbed her around her waist and lifted her up. She laughed until he spun her around and pushed her against an old oak, trapping her wrists in one hand above her head.

"I thought you said you wouldn't run from me again," he said against her lips.

"I knew you'd catch me." Belle closed the distance between them, licking his lower lip.

He kissed her lips, her cheeks, her jaw. Buried his face against her neck and breathed deeply. "You make me lose my mind, Beauty," he growled against her. He pushed a leg between hers and placed his free hand on her throat, keeping her pinned against the tree. "I can't get you out of my head."

He stepped back and looked at Belle, standing against the tree, her hands still over her head, panting hard.

"Take off your clothes." For a heartbeat, he thought she would refuse, but then her hands went to her shirt. "Slowly," he ordered when she looked like she was just gonna pull it off. A blush spread on her face, and a wicked smile tugged at his lips. After everything they had been through and done, he loved that she still

172

blushed.

Belle slowly removed her clothes, and for each inch of skin that was revealed, his cock grew harder. When she stood naked against the tree, he itched to go lick every part of her. He wanted to feast on her until she fell apart under his hands, and then when he had put her back together, he wanted to do it all over.

"On your knees, Beauty." His voice was rough with need, and when she dropped to her knees and looked up at him through her lashes, her good eye shining with lust, he was nearly undone. He walked towards her, undoing his pants and grabbing his cock, slowly pumping his hand up and down it a few times.

"Open up, Beauty. Let me use that pretty mouth of yours." He ran his thumb over her bottom lip, waiting for her to decide. She studied his face before her gaze shifted to his cock. She slowly licked her lips. Beast groaned as her hot breath shifted over him and then the soft touch of her tongue against his sensitive head.

"Just like that," he said when she closed her lips around him. He fought to stay still, to let her explore at her own tempo.

Her movements were unsure, and when she tried to take more of him, she gagged and pulled away, coughing.

Blood rushed in Beast's ears, and he leaned forward, resting one hand against the tree, and tangled the other in her hair.

"Gods, you sound so good, gagging on my cock, Beauty. I want to grab your face and fuck that pretty little mouth." He pressed his cock against her lips again, and she opened for him. "I want to make you gag and choke on me." He kept her head still and pushed into her waiting heat. "Keep your eyes on me, Beauty. I want to see the tears."

She looked up at him, lust and trust brimming in her eyes. He pushed forward, slow and steady, letting her get used to his size.

"Play with yourself. I want to see you fall apart with my cock in your mouth. I want to feel your moans against me."

Belle didn't even hesitate to do as he ordered. Her hand slid over her thighs and to her pussy, and he felt the moans against his cock as her fingers found their mark.

Her other hand grabbed his thigh, her nails digging into the fabric of his pants as he pushed deeper. But not even when tears started to run down her face did she look away from him. She was the most beautiful thing he had ever seen.

"Fuck, you do this so well, Beauty. And don't worry, I'll teach you to take it all one day." He growled, and she sucked him harder, her tongue pressing against his cock, adding more sensation to what was already heaven.

Shivers shook her body, and her mouth went slack around him as she moaned loudly when she came. His balls drew up, and he used his hold on her hair to pull her to her feet. He wanted to be buried deep in her pussy when he came.

He didn't care about the spit on her chin as he slammed his lips on hers. He tasted himself on her tongue and groaned deep as he grabbed her thighs and lifted her, slamming her back against the tree. Her

174

pussy was wet and warm, and he slid to the hilt with a groan. He fucked her hard and rough, her body taking everything he gave. Her nails bit into his shoulders as he roared his release.

His legs were unsteady, and he eased out of Belle before taking them both to the ground, cradling her against his chest. He sat against the tree and wiped Belle's face with his shirt sleeve.

"Are you okay?" he asked. He hadn't meant to be quite as rough, but Belle kept meeting everything head on, and then demanding more. It drove him to break free of the steel rules that had controlled his life for so many years.

"Perfect," she grinned up at him. "Maybe I need to run some more."

"If you keep running from me, I might have to tie you up."

Belle laughed and leaned her head back against his chest. He buried his face in her hair and inhaled and smelled fresh blood.

"You're bleeding," he said and frowned at her.

"It's nothing. Just a few scratches."

"Where?" he demanded and received an eye roll in answer. Not satisfied, he stood and put Belle on her feet. She crossed her arms and glared at him.

"Really? A few scratches and you ruin my glow?"

Beast looked at her from head to toe but couldn't see anything. He grabbed her shoulders, turned her, and found scrapes all over her back where the tree's rough bark had rubbed against her skin.

Belle grabbed his face and made him look at her. "I

appreciate the concern, but we both know I'll be healed in a few hours." She smirked up at him. "And that we've given each other worse wounds than that." She ran her fingers over the bite on his neck, and he shivered against her.

"Sorry," he breathed against her lips and kissed her before pulling her into his embrace.

"You're funny sometimes," Belle said.

"How?" he asked.

"Sometimes you act all protective and dominant, and at the same time, you let me fight against a monster."

Beast raised an eyebrow. "I'm pretty sure I told you not to fight the monster. But Belle, you're a grown woman, and no matter how I feel, you are capable of taking care of yourself. You're not a frail human girl. If you want to run headlong into danger, it's not my job to stop you."

"Thank you," she said and hugged him closer.

"Just don't ask me to stand back. I will be right there, by your side, doing my best to protect you."

"I know," she said and stepped back. She grabbed her clothes, and while she got dressed, he righted his own clothes. The sun had set, and they needed to get back to camp before the fire burned down.

Chapter 19

Belle pulled the hood further over her head as they rode through the town's gates. The plan was to get supplies and information about the monsters and the lost prince. They were so far away from her little village that the rumors about Belle shouldn't have reached the town, but she was still nervous. Despite her new powers, she didn't want people to attack her.

They left the horses at one of the temporary stables, paying a coin to the stable boy to bring them water and hay. Beast extended his arm to Belle, and she took it, and together they walked to the market. Once again, she was overwhelmed by everything on display. But this time, everything was so much more. Staying at the castle, and riding in the woods, hadn't quite prepared her for how much her senses had enhanced. Every sound was too loud. The scents assaulted her nose, and there were so many she couldn't shift through them.

A seller yelled next to her, and Belle flinched at the sound.

"Deep breaths, Belle. You're just a little nervous, and that's making everything worse. Let your beast sort through the scents and sounds," Beast whispered against her ear.

Belle took a few deep breaths and called on her beast a little. The sensations didn't lessen, but they felt less forceful with the beast to help. It wasn't a perfect fix, but she felt like she could breathe again. He was right. She was nervous, and her body wound up tight, expecting something bad to happen. She forced herself to relax and smiled up at him.

Beast gave her a quick kiss and led her to a stall where they could buy the first of their supplies.

The inn was busy, and Belle was glad for the shadows that offered her some measure of privacy in the corner of the room. Beast sat beside her, his back against the wall so he could keep an eye on everything. The serving girl placed two mugs of ale and two bowls of stew, and Belle's mouth watered. Her beast was happy eating roasted meat every night, but she missed herbs and potatoes. Beast apparently had a contact in town that was supposed to meet them there. She guessed he'd made many connections over a couple of hundred years.

And yet, he seemed to keep himself apart from the world. She thought of all the people he would have lost. The people he would have seen grow old and die while he stayed the same. She had seen the way he looked at the Potters with sorrow.

Would she end up like him? Watching everyone she cared about die? She grabbed his hand, and he smiled at her. They had each other, and that was enough.

They were halfway through the stew when a man sat down beside Belle. He was a giant compared to her and easily stood a head above Beast. Short hair and a neatly trimmed beard gave him a gentle face, but his body was massive, carrying muscles that threatened to rip the seams of his shirt. The man gave her a big smile which faltered when he noticed the scars and the white eye. That close, even the shadows and her hood couldn't hide them. She lifted her lip in a silent growl and met his surprised eyes head-on.

The man quickly looked away, and Belle saw the laugh in Beast's eyes as he extended a hand to the man.

"Matthew, this is my companion."

The man grabbed Beast's hand but studied her with a new interest.

"So, what's new?" Beast asked when it seemed Matthew wasn't going to talk on his own. The man looked at Beast, but only for a few seconds before he looked down at the table. Belle frowned. Was the man afraid of Beast?

"There's been talk about a monster in the woods only a few days from here."

"It's dead," Belle said with a bit of satisfaction.

"Good." The man looked around them and leaned in closer. "The message said you wanted information about the lost princes?"

Beast nodded.

"There's a rumor that the youngest prince disappeared a few days ago on his fifteenth birthday. Soldiers have searched the whole town and the woods, but no official reason has been given. It's a hundred years since the last prince disappeared, and the crown is, according to rumors, of course, nervous the people will think them cursed."

Adrenalin shot through Belle. The witch had to be close if there was a new lost prince. Beast's face stayed impassive, and Matthew didn't linger. He gave them both a polite nod and left their table. Beast threw a few coins on the table, and Belle gave the rest of her stew a sad glance before following him outside.

"Why didn't Matthew meet your eyes?" she asked as they walked down a side street. Beast glanced at her before looking back at their surroundings. He had been doing that ever since they entered the city. He didn't seem scared, but he was alert and on guard.

"No one meets my eyes. Except you."

"What do you mean?" she asked.

"Human instinct tells them not to look a predator in the eyes." He laughed a little. "Well, except for you. Even as a kid, you looked me straight in the eyes when I rescued you."

"Are you saying I have a bad survival instinct?" she asked with a laugh.

"No, I'm saying you're the bravest person I've met."

Belle hid her smile in her hood. She liked knowing he thought her brave.

"Will people stop looking me in the eyes, too?" she asked. She wasn't sure how she felt about that. If she saw her father again, would he look away from her eyes? Would some unexplainable instinct tell him she was dangerous?

"They already avoid it," Beast answered.

"No, they don't. Matthew stared straight into my eyes."

"No, you caught him in your gaze."

180

"What's the difference?" she asked.

"When someone looks you in the eyes, they are deliberately making contact. You were angry with Matthew for staring at your scars and looked into his eyes while growling at him. His instinct told him that you might rip his throat out if he looked away."

Belle grinned at that. She liked that a big man like Matthew could find her dangerous. Even if it wasn't a conscious decision.

They had left the city behind and were riding north. If the newly cursed prince had run off, Beast thought it most likely that he ran up into the mountains. Hopefully, they would be able to catch his scent and follow it.

"What do we do if he's in beast form and not friendly. I don't want to hurt a scared boy," Belle said from Kalon.

"We're two, and I'm a lot scarier than any fifteen-year-old kid could ever be. We can subdue him without hurting him."

They rode for another half hour before Beast caught a scent. He stopped his horse, and Belle stopped beside him. "Do you smell anything?" she asked.

"Maybe." He jumped to the ground and inhaled deeply. The unmistakable scent of beast and magic lingered in the air. Beast looked back the way they had come from. They had ridden for less than an hour.

Could the prince really be hiding this close?

Beast tried to remember the lay of the land, but it had been too long since he had been there, and everything had changed too much.

He swung back in the saddle. "Keep your senses open. He's near."

"What will we do with him when we find him?" Belle asked.

"Talk to him. Explain what is happening."

"And then what? Bring him back to the town?"

Beast shook his head. "We can't take him back. What happens when he shifts at the full moon? Or when he stops aging?"

Belle bit her lower lip. "So, what do we do then? We can't just leave him."

"Let's talk to him, and then we'll figure it out, okay?"

Belle nodded, and Beast gave an internal sigh of relief. He had no idea what to do with the boy or if they could talk him down.

Belle was the one to catch the boy's scent a quarter of an hour later. They had been smelling the trails of men since they left the town, but they had all been days old. Probably the soldiers. Beast figured the boy had run far into the mountains and then come back down when the soldiers left. They left the horses and went on foot. There was no reason to tempt a newly turned beast with the fresh scent of prey.

"There," Beast said and pointed at an outcropping of rocks, forming the entrance to a cave. The smell of beast and magic was so strong it nearly clogged his nose. They crouched at the edge of some bramble bushes and watched for any movement. They would probably have the most luck if they could get to the boy while human.

"The smell is so strong," Belle whispered and wrinkled her nose.

Movement from the cave entrance cut off his response, and they both watched as a beast walked out. It looked miserable. Head hanging low, ears drooping. It was smaller than both Beast and Belle, and it looked as if it hadn't fully grown into its body yet.

They looked at each other before stepping out into the open.

The beast whirled on them with a growl.

"Stop," Beast growled, meeting the beast's gaze. "I know this is confusing, but we're not going to hurt you."

The beast looked between them, still growling but looking more unsure than angry.

"We're here to help you. Can you shift back?" Belle asked, and the beast focused on her. Beast didn't much like it. If anything went wrong, he wanted the beast to focus on him, not Belle, but there wasn't much he could do about it either.

The beast took a small step forward and then collapsed. The body split, folded in on itself, leaving a young boy lying on the ground, panting.

"Here." Belle pulled her cloak off and carefully placed it around the boy's shoulders. Beast loomed over them, but the boy didn't seem to be a danger.

He just looked young and scared. Beast wondered if he had ever been that young and scared? How his life would have looked if someone had found him and explained things to him. If he hadn't spent fifteen years trapped in a rage that made him into a killer.

No one had done that for him, but maybe he could do that for the young prince.

"What's happening to me?" the boy asked and pulled the cloak closer around his naked form.

"You've been cursed," Beast said and knelt down beside the boy. He grabbed the boy's chin and lifted his head. They stared at each other, beast to beast, for a few heartbeats before the boy looked down. "That's good," Beast said. "You aren't letting your beast rule you."

"I can't go home, can I?" the boy said in a broken voice. Belle ran her hand through his hair, and it pulled at Beast's heart. He hoped he wasn't ruining things between them, but he couldn't leave the boy behind. "You'll come with us, and we'll teach you everything we know."

The boy looked between them, unsure, and Belle smiled at him. "I'm Belle, and the growly man is Beast." She stood, and Beast automatically extended his hand to help her. "Come with us to our horses. We'll get you dressed and feed you some real food. Then we can talk."

The boy perked up at the mention of food and got to his feet, doing his best to keep everything covered.

Back at the horses, Belle found some clothes for the boy among Beast's things while he started a fire. The clothes hung on the boy's thin frame, but he seemed pleased to be dressed again.

"So, can you tell us what happened?" Beast asked.

They were sitting around the fire, eating bread, cheese and sweetmeats.

"It happened a few days ago, on my fifteenth birthday. I was getting ready for the celebrations when there was a knock on my door. An old woman, who I had never seen before, came inside. I asked her who she was, and she said she was just a humble servant." The boy frowned and pulled a face that said he clearly hadn't believed her. "I know every servant working in the private rooms. She was not one of them. She laughed at me and said that I'd have to pay for the sins of my fathers." He swallowed and put down the food he'd been enjoying. Shivers ran through his body.

Beast felt an overwhelming need to protect this boy, even knowing there was no one to protect him from.

"She touched my forehead, and the next thing I remember is running around in the forest as some kind of monster." The boy hugged himself.

"Beast, not a monster," Belle said.

"What?" the boy asked.

"You're a beast," Beast said. "Monsters are terrible things trapped between human and beast. Raving mad and unable to change to either form."

"Where do the monsters come from?" the boy asked in a whisper.

"If we bite a human while in our beast shape, we infect them," Belle explained.

"And you're both…"

"Beasts? Yes."

"Were you cursed too?"

"I was. A couple of hundred years ago." Beast said.

The boy paled, and Belle gave him a sour look. Beast raised an eyebrow at her. What did she want him to do? Lie?

"We're not quite sure what happened to me," Belle said, pointedly ignoring Beast's silent question.

"So, what happens to me now?" the boy asked in a small voice.

"You'll come with us," Belle said, smiling at the boy. Beast didn't miss the worried glance she gave him, and he gave her a quick nod in agreement.

"We have plenty of room, and you can learn to control your new powers. When you get older, you can decide if you want to travel out into the world or stay," Beast said, leaving no room for arguments. It was too dangerous to have a freshly cursed monster running free this close to a town.

"Did the witch say anything about true love? Or give you a rose?" Beast asked.

"Last night. I woke in the cave, and she was standing before me. I was in the other shape, and it was so confusing that all I could do was growl at her."

"I had it the same way. I wanted to yell at him." Belle nodded at Beast. "And all I did was make weird growly noises."

Belle and the boy both laughed, and Beast couldn't help his smile.

"She told me I had five years to find true love, and then she left a rose on the ground and just disappeared." The boy licked his lips. "What does that mean? Finding true love?"

Beast shook his head. "I don't know. When I was cursed, I was so consumed with anger I spent fifteen years fighting in wars. When I got back home, the rose was dead."

Belle looked at him. "Do you think she's still around? Also, why did she curse the same royal house twice? I've not read about that happening before."

"I don't know. She can blink in and out of existence for all we know." Beast broke a stick in two and fed the pieces to the flames.

"There's a haunted witch's house in these mountains," the boy said.

Beast looked at him. "There are so-called witch's houses all over the continent. Every time a woman speaks her mind, someone will shout witch."

The boy nodded in agreement. "True, but I've read the accounts. A woman and her daughter lived in the mountains and were renowned as wise women. But then the daughter fell in love with a married man, and his wife got sick." The boy looked between them. "I'm not saying she actually cursed her, but she died, and the townspeople burned her as a witch. According to the records, the mother stayed in the house, but weird things started to happen to people who went near it."

Beast looked at Belle. It was a weak clue, but it was the best they had. If they wanted to find the witch, they might as well start here.

Chapter 20

Belle steered Kalon around the fallen log and glanced at Beast. The boy, Maël, had never ridden before, so he was sitting behind Beast. None of them looked comfortable about the close proximity, but when Belle had suggested Maël could ride behind her, Beast had growled and refused. Maël had been smart enough not to argue.

Belle liked Maël. He was shy and quiet but helped where he could. It was clear he had grown up sheltered, being the youngest prince, but he didn't complain and listened when Belle or Beast explained things to him.

They were getting closer to where the witch was rumored to live, and Belle had a bad feeling in the pit of her stomach. Something was watching them, and Belle felt like the forest was following their every move.

Beast and Maël looked tense, and the horses were snorting at the shadows. Belle drew the big knife Beast had given her and rested it against her thigh. If something did come out of the shadows, they wouldn't get a chance to attack Kalon.

They came to a fork in the narrow path they were following. One led up the mountain, the other along the mountainside.

Every instinct in her body told her to go up the mountain, that following that path was the right thing to do. But she could smell the magic in the air, so she turned Kalon towards the other path, even as her beast began clawing at her to go the other way.

"No, no," Maël screamed behind her, and she turned in time to see him slip off Agathon. Beast cursed and jumped off too, and she watched as they disappeared between the trees.

The sound of ripping clothes and then the snarls of beasts came from between the trees, and Belle gritted her teeth. There was nothing she could do to help. Someone had to stay with the horses in this cursed place. She turned Kalon around and grabbed Agathon's reins.

Belle kept her eyes on the forest around her, aware that she was the perfect target. Alone with two horses, while Beast and Maël were off in the trees. If anything were to attack them, this would be their best chance.

Something moved to her left, hidden in the underbrush. A branch snapped. Low panting. She slid off Kalon and grabbed both sets of reins in one hand. She couldn't allow the horses to run. She slowly turned, trying to track whatever was out there on sound alone.

A growl trickled towards her. Not the growl of a beast but something else. The small hairs on her arms stood up as the growl was answered by three voices. The wind shifted, and the stench of wolf filled her nose. But something was wrong with them. Twisted. They smelled of death.

She turned slightly when something emerged from the shadows, trying to keep her eyes on everything else.

It had once been a wolf. It still had patches of fur, but most of its flesh was rotting off the bones, leaving open wounds dripping putrid blood and puss. It looked at her with dead eyes, spit hanging from its open jaws and dripping to the forest floor.

Belle fought the urge to gag and back up with the horses. She wanted to let go of them because fighting one-handed with two panicking horses pulling at her was going to be almost impossible, but if they ran, she risked some of the monster wolves hunting them.

The wolf moved closer, and another one came out of the shadows. She gripped her knife harder, then relaxed her grip a little. She tried to slow her racing heart, but she wasn't stupid. Her situation was nearly impossible.

She swung the blade with all her enhanced strength and sliced into the neck of the wolf who had jumped at her. More putrid blood drenched the forest floor, and she kicked the wolf away. The cut should have killed it, but the wolf was already dead. It didn't even yelp in pain. Just shook its head and staggered back to its feet.

She hadn't seen the third wolf sneak out behind her, and she whirled around as it came at her. But before it hit her, Agathon reared and hit it with his massive hooves. He gave off a stallion's battle scream and trampled the wolf under him. Belle released both horses as more wolves stepped forward. Neither

Agathon nor Kalon seemed inclined to run, and with this many wolves, she needed both hands and a lot of luck.

The wolf she had cut came back for round two, and Belle took a lesson from Agathon. The wolf he had trambled didn't move. Maybe what she needed was brute strength. She dropped the knife, picked up a heavy branch, and slammed it into the side of the wolf's head. A satisfying crunch came from the impact, and the wolf collapsed to the ground.

Belle smiled as she turned towards the rest of the wolves. She could do this. She could save herself and the horses.

Beast watched as Maël disappeared between the trees. His beast wanted to give chase, but he had already left Belle alone for too long. Whatever magic the witch used to keep people away from her home, it hit Maël hard. Beast had tried to stop him and had gotten claws and teeth as a reply. They would just have to find the boy when the witch was dead. Most likely, he would run right back to the caves they had found him at the first time.

He shifted back to human and walked towards the path they had followed. He was near the spot where he had left Belle when a sour stench hit him. Wolf and rotting flesh filled his nose, and he took off at a run, his heart hammering in his chest. He ignored the branches and thorny berry bushes that ripped at his naked flesh, focused only on returning to Belle. He should never have left her alone. He had smelled the magic. Had known something was watching them.

He stumbled to a halt when he hit the path. Belle stood with a branch gripped in one hand. Putrid blood dripped off her arms and was splattered over her face and shirt. Both horses stood behind her. Wild-eyed but snorting in anger. And all around her were the remains of undead wolves. Beast did a quick headcount. Eleven.

Belle saw him, and a huge smile spread on her lips. She looked him up and down, and her smile dimmed. When she looked behind him and saw that Maël wasn't with him, the smile turned into a frown.

"You're hurt. What happened? Where's Maël?" she asked.

"I could ask the same." Beast looked pointedly at the dead wolves.

"The witch or I'm assuming it was the witch, sent her little pawns after us. I stopped them."

"I can see. Are you alright?"

"I'm fine. I can't say the same about you, though. What happened?"

"The magic got to Maël. I tried to stop him, and he shifted. He ended up running away."

Beast pulled Belle close and hugged her, ignoring the nauseous stench clinging to her. She dropped the branch and hugged him back.

"I'm sorry I left you," he said.

"I'm not. Maël is just a kid. He needed you. Besides, I can take care of myself."

192

"I know. But you shouldn't have to."

Belle gave him a quick smile before it fell again. "Should we go after Maël?"

"No. Let's take care of the witch first. I'm pretty sure he's running straight back to those caves. He'll be safer there than here with us."

Belle nodded, then stepped back. "I stink, and now you got it all over you too." She sighed and tried to wipe her hands on her shirt.

"There's a small pond not far from here. Let's wash up." He grabbed the reins, and Belle followed him to the water. She started out trying to clean her clothes but gave up and took them off. Beast stood in the water and watched her. Even covered in rotting blood, he had never seen anyone as beautiful as her. He didn't care that scars covered her body. In his mind, they were a road map that he could follow to explore her. They showed her strength and stubbornness.

They were dressed and back on the horses. The magic in the air was pressing down on them as a heavy blanket, trying to smother them in fear. Beast constantly had to fight a growl, and he kept glancing around them to make sure nothing was attacking them. Belle's hands were fisted tightly around the reins, and her face was bloodless. He couldn't imagine how hard this had to be for her. He had a lot more practice keeping his beast under control.

"This witch really doesn't want visitors," Belle said in a strained voice. Beast nodded, not in any state to form a full sentence. If they didn't reach the witch's house soon, they might have to give up because his beast was trying to rip him to pieces.

They rode another ten minutes, but it felt like hours, every second its own form of torture. The horses suddenly planted their feet and refused to move. Beast swore and jumped to the ground. Belle did the same, every movement tight and controlled as if she was afraid that if she relaxed even the tiniest bit, she would lose it.

They walked side by side, and each step was a fight. A fight against the fear that screamed at him to grab Belle and run, and a fight against his beast that ripped at his insides.

He reached out blindly and grabbed Belle's hand, focusing on her touch, using it to keep moving.

"I, I can't," Belle whispered on a growl. Panic beat at him. If she ran, he would lose it too. But this was their chance to stop the witch. Beast did the only thing he could think of and pulled her close. She was his, and the witch had no hold on her. He took her in a feral kiss, his fingers digging into her flesh, claiming her back from the magic. Belle pressed against him, one hand pulling his hair, the other digging into his chest, sending lightning of pain and pleasure through him. He pulled back and leaned his head against hers, panting hard. His thoughts felt cloudy, tinged with lust, but the overwhelming need to run was gone.

"Better?" he asked.

"Yeah. It feels like I can breathe again." Belle pulled his hair, and he leaned down to give her another kiss. She tasted sweet, her lips soft and pliant. The hard edge of the scar cleaving through her lips added another layer of sensation. He groaned and pulled her closer. He wanted to rip her clothes off. To feast on her body until she screamed his name.

The sensation of being watched shivered across his back, and he reluctantly pulled away from Belle's embrace.

"I'm going to kill that witch," Belle growled, and for the first time since they took this path, Beast laughed. Trust his little savage Beauty to bring a smile to his lips.

Chapter 21

The small cottage lay nestled between the tall trees. The roof was covered in green grasses and soft moss, and the windows were dark gaping holes, ready to suck you inside. Belle eyed it carefully, but there was no sign of anything living. The clearing in front of the house was quiet, too quiet. No insects buzzing. No leaves rustling.

"Something is really wrong here," Belle said, glancing at the forest around them.

"I feel it too," Beast said. He picked up a stone, and Belle followed its path through the air and watched it bounce on the ground. When nothing happened, Belle looked at Beast.

"Got any more cool tricks?" She asked, her lips quirking up despite the magic beating on her.

Beast shook his head and stepped forward, and Belle followed.

Each step closer to the cottage made it feel like the air was sticking to her skin. She had an overwhelming need to scratch her skin to remove the suffocating feeling.

Beast doubled over beside her, his knees hitting the ground hard. He clawed at his face, and she watched, horrified, and it started to split apart.

"Beast?" she screamed and fell to her knees beside him, though she had no idea what to do. His skin was being carved up by an unseen power. She inhaled and nearly choked on magic. The witch. She had to be close.

Belle grabbed her knife and jumped to her feet. She slowly turned, looking for anything that might reveal the witch's hiding place.

Belle clamped her hands over her ears as a loud pop grated against her brain. The sticky air broke apart, and Belle blinked against the new scene in front of her.

The cottage looked the same, but the ground around it lay dead and bare. Poles had been hammered into the earth, carrying torches to dispel the darkness, and skulls and bones hung from them. The smell of rot was heavy in the air, and Belle tried not to stare too long at the half-rotted human face beside her.

A woman, looking no older than Belle, stood at the door to the cottage. She wore a simple brown dress, and her long blond hair was tied back from her face. She was pretty, with blue eyes and slim features. The only mark on her seemed to be the angry red scar of a cross on her forehead.

"Let him go," Belle said and pointed her knife at the witch. She took a step to the side, trying to shield Beast. He was whimpering and screaming, and the scent of blood was heavy in the air.

"Why? I made him. It's only fitting I become his death."

"No," Belle growled. Beast was hers, and there was no way she would let this witch take him from her.

The witch frowned at her. "Who are you, girl?"

"I'm the girl whose life was destroyed because of your curse."

"I never cursed you."

"No, you didn't. But I'm cursed all the same."

The witch shook her head. "The curse is for men and men only."

"Men? You curse children who have done nothing wrong."

"Nothing wrong? My daughter was fifteen when they burned her for witchcraft. She was an innocent child."

"So what? This is revenge?"

"As long as men burn innocent women, I will curse their sons."

"And what about the women and children your monsters kill? What about my mother, who was killed by one of your monsters?"

The witch looked shocked, as if she had never even thought about that possibility. "They are the mothers of hatred and discrimination," she finally said with determination.

Belle pointed at Beast. "He never did anything wrong. You're sick."

"Why do you care so much?" the witch asked.

"Because... because I love him."

"Love?" the witch laughed. "The rose is dead. There's no true love for him anymore. All you could ever be is a weak imitation."

Belle was so angry tears ran down her cheeks.

"Can a beast really love? Are you sure it's not just possession?" the witch asked.

"I love him, and he loves me." The torches nearest her roared as her power grabbed hold of the flames.

"What are you?" the witch asked, eying the flames.

"My name is Belle Rose, and I'll break every curse you've ever placed on an innocent person." Belle grabbed the fire and fed all her anger, fear, and despair into it. It hurtled to the witch, and the woman took the flames in the chest. The force pushed her into the gaping mouth of the cottage, and Belle threw herself over Beast as fire exploded out of the cottage, ripping it apart.

"Beast?"

Beast blinked and tried to think through the ringing in his ears. Pain crashed through him as a wave caught in a bottle, moving back and forth. He coughed, and blood filled his mouth.

"The witch," he hissed and tried to push up from the ground. He collapsed back on the ground with a groan when his body refused to follow his orders.

"Don't move," Belle's voice sounded frantic. He tried to focus on her face, on anything, but all he got was a blur.

"The witch is dead." A sob choked her voice. "I need to get this bleeding stopped. There's so much blood."

"What happened?" he forced the words to form, and they came out scratchy and raw.

199

"The witch did something with her magic, and it ripped you apart. I can't get the bleeding to stop. You need to shift. You can't die, you hear me? I won't allow it."

The pain had finally ebbed a little, and he started to feel his body again. It had almost been better when he had just been in a sea of pain. Now he felt everything. The fire in his chest. How one lung seemed to refuse to fill with air. His left arm twitched, and the right didn't seem to move at all. The sticky feeling of blood covered him.

He realized that it wasn't his eyes that didn't work. They were just filled with blood.

"You need to shift."

Beast tried to refuse, but his tongue had stopped obeying his command. Shifting while this hurt would be too dangerous. The most likely scenario was him ending up dead. Worst case scenario, his beast would be in control and kill everything.

Strong fingers grabbed his face, and Belle's sweet lips brushed over his. Salt dripped onto his useless tongue, and he realized she was crying.

"Please, Beast. You're dying. I can't do this without you. Please, please shift."

He reached deep inside him and released the beast. Had he been more alert, more in his right mind, he would never have done it with Belle so close. But he wasn't in his right mind, and the shift tore into him.

He roared as his skin knit and his lung filled with air once more. Nerves burned as muscles reattached and bones realigned. He stumbled to his feet, then collapsed to his side, heaving against the pain.

He blinked and focused on Belle crouched in front of him. She was watching him closely, her body tight and ready. Blood covered big parts of her, but his nose told him it was mostly his. Behind her, the cottage stood in flames, and a few trees had caught fire too.

He stayed lying on the ground until the pain became manageable. He wanted to go to Belle. To reassure her that he was fine. But right that second, he wasn't sure that that wasn't a blatant lie. He forces himself into an upright position. He wasn't yet clearheaded enough to stand up, but he could at least lie with most of his body off the ground.

"We need to get you some food," Belle said and straightened. She looked around them and shook her head. Beast had noticed it too. There wasn't so much as a scent trail near them. The witch's magic had held everything at bay.

"Can you move?"

Beast shook his head. It would take some time before he could move from his spot. As it was, he was lucky to be alive.

"Okay, wait here, and I'll try and hunt something."

He noticed a trembling in her hands as she tried to pull the shirt over her head. He gave her a closer look. She looked thinner. As if whatever she had done to stop the witch had sucked energy right out of her body. She slowly undressed, her skin split, and her beast spilled forth. She shook off the effects of the shift, gave him a lick across his bloody nose, and ran between the trees.

Beast put his head on the ground and closed his eyes. He was so tired, the world was spinning, and everything hurt. But they did it. They killed the witch. There would be no more cursed princes.

Rustling came from the forest, and he growled low. If he was attacked, there was no way he could defend himself. But it wasn't an enemy. Belle bounded over, a deer clamped in her jaws. She dropped it in front of him and sat back, looking at him expectantly.

He sank his teeth deep, ripped off a big chunk of meat, and tossed it to Belle. He looked at her expectantly until she started to eat. Satisfied, he tore into the meat, letting the warmth and blood slide over his tongue and feed him the energy he so desperately needed.

When they were both full, Belle lay down beside him and tucked her head against his neck. He sighed and inhaled her scent. Even as a beast, she smelled of Belle. Of home and flowers.

Beast woke naked and cold. Everything was sore, but the persistent pain had faded away. Belle was sprawled across his chest, and her little snores blew feather kisses across his neck. He inhaled deeply and relished that he could do so without the crippling pain. He ran his hands through Belle's thick hair, and she stirred against him.

"Hey," he said and kissed her forehead.

"How are you feeling?" she asked and sat up.

"Much better. Food and shifting helped."

"Good." She looked at him with fire burning in her eyes. "I thought I had lost you. If you ever do that to me again…" her voice trailed off as tears mixed with her anger.

"I promise not to go hunt any more witches," he chuckled and pulled her into his lap.

"It's not funny," she growled and slapped his chest.

"I know. I'm sorry."

"Just don't die."

"I won't. And I'm sorry the curse didn't break."

"I'm not. Together, we can do so much with this." Belle reached out and a flame jumped from one of the still-burning torches to her fingers. They watched it dance against her skin for a few seconds before she closed her hand, killing the flame.

"You've gotten good at that," Beast commented.

"I got so angry, I didn't even think when I burned the witch. It was like something just clicked inside me."

"Did you put out the fire?" The cottage and some of the trees were smoldering ruins, but there wasn't any more fire.

"Yeah. I was afraid it would burn down the mountain."

"Good." He hugged her close before letting her go. He finally felt like he could move and had no interest in staying longer than needed in the witch's clearing. She might be dead, but so was the land beneath them. It felt all wrong, and the little hairs on his body stood up just thinking about it.

Belle helped him to stand and then put on her clothes. Beast had nothing to cover with. The shift had torn his clothes, and what was left was covered in dried blood. Resigned to trekking through the forest naked, he let Belle help him hobble down the forest path. "Let's go find the boy, and go home."

"Home, I like that." Belle sounded tired, but there was a happy note in her voice as she said it.

"You saved my life," he told her.

"And you've saved mine. I think that makes us even." She smiled big at him, and Beast felt a lightness he hadn't felt since he was a small kid.

"I do believe I saved you three times. You still owe me two." He winked at her, and she scowled up at him.

"If you put me into a situation like this again, there won't be a third time because I'll have killed you before that."

Beast laughed. He would never get tired of his savage Belle, who saw the beauty in his beast.

ABOUT THE AUTHOR

Tea Spangsberg lives in the south of Denmark on a small island with her family. She claims to be a Viking but would be rubbish at it as she gets terribly seasick, but let's not tell anyone.

Her parents taught her the love of reading from an early age, and she grew up surrounded by books. Her love for reading morphed into the need to tell her own stories, and she never looked back. Reading still plays a big part in her life, and she loves everything from fantasy to crime fiction.

When it comes to writing, her big love is fantasy, but she often dabbles in other genres and delights in writing everything from flash fiction to novels.

She might have a slight addiction to coffee, sharp-edged objects, and books of a peculiar nature.

Read more about her published and upcoming books on www.teaspangsberg.com

Made in the USA
Las Vegas, NV
10 May 2023